A MALICIOUS SUMMER VACATION

A STANDALONE HOLIDAY PARANORMAL ROMANCE

MONSTERS OF THE DIVIDE
BOOK 3

T. B. WIESE

Cover design by GetCovers

Chapter art by T. B. Wiese in Canva Pro

ISBN: 978-1-959657-15-6 ebook

ISBN: 978-1-959657-14-9 paperback

BOOKS IN THIS WORLD

- Paine for the Holidays
- A Vexing Valentines
- A Malicious Summer Vacation
- Hunted on Halloween (coming fall 2024)

Make the time for you.
Take a walk in the sun.
Enjoy a good meal.
Read a good book.

AUTHOR'S NOTE

**Please take care of yourself and your mental health

A Malicious Summer Vacation is an ADULT paranormal romance that contains elements such as: monsters, violence, swearing, stalking (and not the morally grey main character kind us dark romance readers like - this is real world stalking that's creepy bordering on dangerous), blood, gore, being cut - on purpose and by accident, removal and consuming eyeballs, biting, claiming, and sexually explicit scenes ... with monsters.

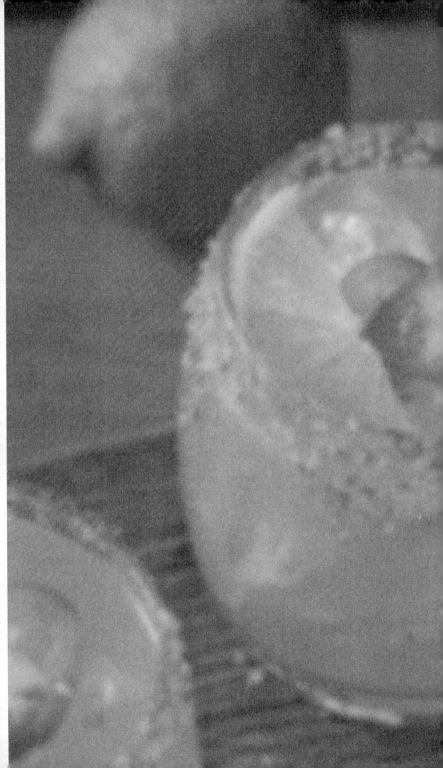

SUMMER'S SPICY MARGARITAS

The Ingredients

• **Tequila** 1 oz. Summer uses anjeo (aged) for the strongest flavor. Be generous with your pour, and if it isn't strong enough once mixed, you can always top off.

• **Lime Juice 2 oz**. Summer demands you USE FRESH!

• **Orange Juice 2 oz**. This adds a bright, citrusy flavor, and allows you to use less sweetener since the orange juice lends natural sugars.

• **Agave 1/2 oz**. A touch of sweetness to balance the spicy and smooth out the tequila. Add to your preference.

• **Jalapeño**. Slice it up. Take the seeds out if you're looking for less heat. Muddle in the shaker if you want more heat infused in your drink.

• **Tajin salt + Lime Wedge**. Salting the rims creates a beautiful (and tasty!) presentation. Summer uses a mix of Tajin spice and sea salt for a little extra spice.

The Directions

1 Rim It. Rim the glass and fill it with ice.

2 Shake It. Add the spicy margarita recipe ingredients and ice to a cocktail shaker. Shake for 30 seconds, then strain into the glass. Feel free to add those jalapeño slices to your glass. ENJOY!

MONSTERS OF THE DIVIDE

*Most of these are only briefly mentioned in passing, so don't feel too overwhelmed.

Nepha (Our MMC) - *Humanoid with metallic feathered wings. These are the creatures Angles were modeled from. They are exceptional hunters - even our MMC is wary of them. They are beautiful but cruel. Most believe that if they have hearts, they are made of stone.*

Dremar - *Think vampire and gargoyle. This species has different colored skin. Our MMC has blue-grey skin that is smooth and hairless, but others have shades of red or green or black ... Eyes to match their skin color. Males and females have curly horns like an antelope. They are very fast on foot, even faster when flying. They have bat-like wings, a snake-like tail, fangs, and claws. They drink blood, not to survive, but to obtain power. They heal very quickly. Any being that they've tasted the blood of, they can incinerate with a thought. The dremar, but especially our MMC, are feared by other monsters.*

Anza - Smaller comparatively in the monster realm - about the size of the average human female. They have shimmery skin like starlight. They are pretty and disarming. They are one of the fastest monsters, able to move so quickly they are a blur. They have sharp teeth, a hypnotizing gaze, and can secrete hallucinogens from their skin to incapacitate their prey, which they like to peel and eat. Death by anza is very slow and painful. Not only can they heal themselves, but they can heal others - if you can convince them to.

Xani - Scaled skin that is very tough. Hairless. Usually green but can be other colors. They have reflective, reptile-like eyes. Sharp teeth. Extremely fast. Can walk upright or on all fours. They have snake-like tails, and hate the light, always sticking to shadows unless the hunt of a prey brings them out.

Joteunn - Fur-covered like a werewolf, only they don't shift. They have wolf-like ears and a snout with sharp teeth and fangs. They are pretty large comparatively in the monster world and are extremely strong. They heal very quickly as long as they have the magic to do so. They occasionally run in packs but prefer to hunt solo (as most monsters do). They do howl and bark to communicate, though they also speak.

Grateslung - Snake-like creature with the bottom half of a snake, the top half looks like a gargoyle without wings. Stone-like skin on the body, scaled skin on the lower half. Usually shades of grey or black but can be different colors. Their saliva is venomous, and they are very strong and fast.

Quilen - Tall, humanoid monster that's thin but muscled. They have branch-like horns that look too heavy to hold up.

They are dark skinned with black eyes, long spindly fingers with claws. They aren't the fastest of monsters, but they are strong and can slip between shadows.

Grae - Feathered all over. Humanoid body with a sharp beak, eagle talons for feet, and wings for arms. They are not the smartest monster - they are more animalistic.

Hellhounds - Large dog-like creatures the size of a pony. They do not speak. They hunt in packs, but once their prey is caught, it's every hellhound for themselves. They are a little further down on the food chain in the monster realm, which is why they tend to stay in groups.

Unicorns - They look just like our myths. Horse-like creatures with a single horn. But these unicorns are carnivorous with serrated teeth, razor sharp hooves, and are so strong, they can cave in a monster's chest with one kick. Their horns also emit a strong electric shock that can incapacitate or even kill.

Menace - spider like monsters with blades for legs. Hairy. Can't see well. Relies on sound waves and sense of smell. They lay eggs like spiders and shoot webs.

Oulurs - humans call them Oni. Demon-like. Red or black skin with horns and tusks and pointed tails. They will eat anything. Monster. Human. Animal. Plant. Garbage ...

We might meet more monsters in the upcoming books in this series, but these are all the ones in this story.
    Enjoy.

CHAPTER 1

THE SIXTY SECONDS THAT CHANGED THE WORLD

Monsters are real.

Seventy-two years ago, they came.

Supposedly, at first, everyone thought it was a hoax. But it didn't take long for the world to realize that what was happening was indeed real. You can still find old clips of videos people took on their phones that night.

The monsters came through what we now call The Divide—the invisible barrier that separated our realm from theirs. Apparently, all throughout history, the occasional monster would get through—those folktales of werewolves, vampires, and fae started from somewhere. But that night, they all just ... appeared. So many humans lost their lives. The monsters took what they wanted ... blood, bones, fear, souls. Weapons didn't work on most of them ... with their tough skin, scales, super speed, wings, regenerative healing ... The humans were no match. It was a bloodbath. Then, six hours after they appeared, they all just vanished.

The entire planet was still reeling from the attack when it happened the next night, and the next. Always at the same time. Always for six hours. It wasn't until almost a week of the occurrences that someone discovered that the first night the monsters came through, all time stood still for one full minute. Clocks ceased ticking, tides froze, the world stopped turning. No one noticed, because well, monsters. And no one really knows how life on earth survived the literal freezing of time. Time hasn't stopped again since that first night, but the monsters still come.

Humanity's saving grace came with the discovery of magic symbols with the power to keep the monsters out. Who discovered it? That truth is buried under wild conjectures, outlandish legends, and fantastical myths. So, who knows?

And here we are. Life goes on. We go about the monster-free hours almost as normally as before, as if we're trying to ignore the nightmare we know is coming with the fall of The Divide every day. But we all know ...

The monsters *are* coming, and if you want to survive, there are only three rules:

Make sure the correct symbols are carved deep into your threshold and every windowsill.

Be sure you recharge the symbols with a few drops of your blood at least once a month to keep the monsters out.

And whatever you do, don't go outside after the final curfew siren.

CHAPTER 2

SUMMER

This feels weird.

Taking a deep breath, I step outside the townhouse rental I'm staying at for the next few weeks. I glance down at the fresh stain of my blood on the engraved metal threshold. I've thought about upgrading my own thresholds and windowsills to metal. It's more expensive at the front end, but you don't have to worry about the carving degrading over time.

Closing and locking the door, I turn on the stoop and tilt my head up. The morning sun warms my face. Where I live, The Divide falls from the morning through the afternoon, so being out at this time of day is ... scary but exhilarating.

My chest expands dramatically as I take another big gulp of air.

A thudding sound to my right has me clutching the railing, ready to bolt back into my rental. I glance over, only to see a man closing the lid on a trash bin. He wipes his hands on his athletic shorts as he walks to one of the other townhouses on this row.

I chuckle to myself as he climbs the steps and disappears inside. I don't know if I'll get used to being out in the morning without jumping at every little sound, but I'm going to try.

My flip-flops slap against the stairs, and I smile. I'm going out for breakfast!

Standing on the sidewalk, I look one way, then the other. Should I order a ride-share? I reach for my little sling bag secured over my chest but drop my hand. No. No phone. Not right now. I'm on vacation.

My smile falls.

That's not the only reason I don't pull out my phone.

Shaking off the fear that starts creeping into my stomach like an oil slick, I start walking. Yesterday, on the ride here from the airport, I'm pretty sure I saw a cute little shopping center. I slide my sunglasses off the top of my head to rest on my nose. The light breeze ruffles my short hair. It feels good. The day is already heating up. I love it. My mom used to joke that she destined me to love the hot weather when she named me Summer.

A pair of birds dance overhead, dipping and spinning in playful swirls before flying off. The sound of the occasional car breaks up the *slap slap* of my sandals beating a rhythm on the sidewalk. I take the time to admire a blooming tree, its branches fanning out to create a canopy with its feathery leaves. Bright yellow flowers sit on top of the clusters of leaves like sunny little crowns.

I shift, automatically reaching for my phone to take a picture, but pause. Why can't I just stand here and enjoy this beautiful tree? Why do I feel compelled to capture it and share it online?

Because you want to share this moment with someone.

6

I may have millions of followers online across my social media accounts, but close, actual friends? I can count them on one hand. And over the past ten years, they've all gotten married, had kids ... We still chat occasionally on text, but our lives are so different now.

I suffer from a loneliness of my own making.

Shaking off my morose thoughts, I move on. Eventually, I see the terracotta roofs of the shopping area, a few tan umbrellas set up on patios, and a fountain surrounded by lush green plants and bright pink hibiscus.

I give myself a mental pat on the back. *See, Summer? You can do things without your phone. You didn't need step-by-step directions to find this place. And you enjoyed the walk. You were present.*

I chuckle as I pick the place I'm going to try for breakfast. A bell chimes as I push open a door to a restaurant called Restaurant. I have no idea what kind of food they serve, but there's a decent number of cars in the parking lot, so it must be fairly popular.

The low murmur of voices greets me as I make my way to a counter at the back of the small space. Nearly all the tables and booths are occupied. I jerk to a stop as a toddler throws her hands up with a squeal, sending bits of food flying. The woman at the table, presumably her mom, grabs the little girl's arm, whispering, "Bailey, no. Food stays on the plate or goes in your mouth."

Walking by, I see the girl's lips quiver, and I brace for an outburst, but the toddler remains quiet. The mother releases the child's arm, and they both turn back to their pancakes.

Mmm. Pancakes. Though what I call a pancake back home would be called a crepe here. Still, the fluffy rounds look mouthwatering—even the torn up, sticky mess in front of that toddler.

I place my order, and the woman behind the counter smiles, handing me a plastic number. "Go on and sit anywhere you like. We'll bring your food out when it's ready."

I smile back, feeling lighter than I have in ... well, a while.

Turning, I make my way towards the door. There's no way I'm enjoying my breakfast inside today. I'm starting my vacation off right, aiming for one of the little tables sitting out on the patio in the sun.

Jerking to a stop, I realize I forgot to order coffee with my food. The travesty! Spinning, my breath leaves me with an *oomph* as I smack into someone.

I stumble back. "Oh! I'm so sorry."

The woman I nearly took out laughs, apologizing at the same time. "I'm sorry. I wasn't paying attention."

Kneeling, I pick up the little plastic number the woman dropped, handing it to her as I say, "No, that was my fault. I forgot to order coffee and was going back to the counter. I shouldn't have stopped in the middle of the walkway."

I brace for the recognition to enter her eyes, feeling my forced smile making its way to my lips. I have a pretty distinct look with my dark hair shaved on the sides, the longer locks on top just brushing my eyebrows. This style makes my green eyes appear even bigger and highlights my cheekbones. My bold style contrasts with my petite stature. I've been called a pixie on more than one occasion. The look plays well on social media.

At that thought, a dark cloud falls over my mood, but it's quickly banished as the woman's smile grows. "I get it. Can't function without the stuff myself." She looks over her shoulder towards the counter. "Hey, honey, make it two coffees." A tall, handsome man smiles at the woman with a nod before turning back to continue placing their order.

She doesn't recognize me. I mean, that's what I was hoping for when I ended up on this overseas vacation, but still, I have followers from all over the world. Followers I'm currently hiding from.

No, not hiding. I'm just taking a break.

The woman faces me again. "Hope you don't mind. I should have asked how you like yours, but I promise, this drink is the best. One of the reasons we come here."

"You didn't have to do that."

She waves me off, stepping to the side as one of the other patrons makes their way to leave. I fidget my weight to one hip, then the other, before I say, "Thanks. This is my first time here, so I'm happy to trust a local."

The woman smiles. "You're in good hands. I promise." She nods towards the patio. "Were you going to sit out there?"

I nod. "I like the heat."

She laughs. "Me too! Paine isn't a fan, but it's my turn to pick the seats, so he'll just have to deal. Join us? Unless you're meeting someone? I'm Mira, by the way."

Mira doesn't wait for my reply, pressing her back to the door, stepping outside as it swings open. Pulled along by her enthusiastic kindness, I follow. It's already warmer than it was just a few minutes ago, and a little sigh escapes my lips as the sun kisses my skin. Mira sits at a table, and I grab a chair across from her, happy for the company.

We both place our numbers on the table, and she leans back, resting her arms on her chair.

"So, you're not from around here." My brow furrows, and she laughs. "You called me a local."

"Oh, yeah." I chuckle. "I'm here on vacation."

Mira tilts her head. "I thought I heard a bit of an

accent. Well, welcome! I hope you've been enjoying yourself so far."

It's on the tip of my tongue to tell her I just arrived, but I simply nod. I need to get better about spilling all my information to anyone I meet. That's what got me in this situation in the first place.

Mira goes on, "But why here? Why not the beach or the mountains or one of the big cities like New York or something?"

The man from before chuckles as he pulls out a chair with a scrape of metal against cement. I am short. Five-two ... on a good day. So, everyone is tall to me. But this man is taaallll.

The sun glints in my eyes, and my heart kicks in panic. I blink, trying to calm my breathing. That was weird. For a second, it looked like there were giant horns curling up from his head.

He places the chair next to Mira's. As he sits, he pulls a ball cap from his back pocket, securing it over his smooth, shaved head. One of his muscled arms goes around the back of Mira's chair, his hand wrapping around her shoulder as he leans in to kiss her temple. I fight to keep a wistful sigh from passing my lips, trying to push down the gnawing loneliness that aches in my chest. The man nuzzles her hair as he says, "Mira, my love, stop badgering the poor woman."

Her cheeks flush, and when the man sits back, keeping his arm around her, Mira smiles at me. "Sorry. This is Paine. Paine, this is ... shit, I didn't get your name."

Paine chuckles again, and I can't help but smile at the sweet couple. I wave off Mira's embarrassment. "It's very nice to meet you both. I'm Summer."

We all pause our conversation as a teenage boy sets our plates and drinks on the table before asking if we need anything else. We all shake our heads, and the kid makes the rounds to the other outdoor tables.

My mouth waters as I spread the melting butter over my stack of pancakes, the smell of vanilla and sugar making me want to do a little happy dance in my seat. Paine slides the glass bottle of syrup my way, and I smile in thanks.

We remain silent as we get ourselves ready to eat, but then Mira, with her fork of eggs halfway to her mouth says, "Well, Summer, I'm sure you have your summer vacation all planned out, but if you want a friend to hang out with while you're here, let me know. In fact, after breakfast, we're going to a great little independent bookstore right around the corner. It's kinda tucked into a secret little alley." She laughs at my frown. "Alley makes it sound shady. It's actually really cute. An arched walkway lined with flowers leads you between a narrow space between two buildings, and then opens up to an adorable courtyard. That's where the bookstore is."

"That sounds amazing. I'd love to go if you don't mind me tagging along."

Mira nods, "Of course! Yay! Book shopping!"

She smiles around her chewing, and Paine eats silently next to her, casting loving looks her way every so often.

So damn cute.

The wistful jealousy I felt earlier melts away. I like them, and their obvious happiness is contagious. I'm at ease with Mira and Paine. Taking a bite of fluffy pancake, I close my eyes. It's so good. I can't believe I'm *outside*, enjoying the sun and eating breakfast at ten in the morning. I could get used to this.

After another bite, Mira asks, "Would you like my number, you know, just in case you want to get together?

Or you can use me as a resource. I know all the good places to eat." Paine chuckles, and Mira slaps him playfully on the shoulder. "Yes, I like good food, and I know where to get a good meal."

I swear Paine's eyes darken as he licks his lips, his gaze on Mira's mouth. Damn. That's hot.

But then I'm struck with a sliver of panic. Mira reaches across the table towards me. She's going to ask for my phone to put in her number. The lie slides from my lips before I have time to think about it. "Sorry. I forgot my phone when I left this morning."

Mira pulls her hand back and looks around. She makes eye contact with the teenage server, waving him over. She asks for a pen, and he gives her one before hurrying off again. Mira grabs a napkin, jots down her number, and hands it to me.

"Here you go. No pressure. I promise I won't intrude on your vacation. Just, you know, text if you need anything."

My smile is genuine as I take the napkin and fold it, slipping it in the pocket of my cut-off jean shorts. "Thank you, Mira. Sincerely. It's comforting knowing someone here."

She smiles, and Paine kisses her temple again, his fingers playing with a pretty, shimmery bracelet around Mira's wrist. We all go back to eating, and even though sweat starts to stick my black tank top to my skin, I'm relaxed. Happy.

A stray thought pops into my mind, and I bite too hard on my fork in anger. I won't let *him* ruin this. No more. I'm setting myself free of him.

MALICIOUS

My lips curl into a little mischievous smile as I enter the small shop. The smell of coffee almost overwhelms the scent of books as I make my way to the back of the bookstore. I find myself making unnecessarily wide turns around bookshelves, leaving room for the wings that aren't there. Every time I slip this glamour on, my back aches from missing the weight of my black-tipped bronze metal wings. But it's worth it to be here right now.

Yesterday ... I felt *something*. There was a tingling on my skin, an awareness brushing against my brain. Like a memory that won't quite solidify, or like a name you know but can't recall. It lasted just a few moments, but it was enough to pique my interest. So, I decided to come to the human realm to ... investigate if for no other reason than it's something to do—something to dull the never-ending boredom.

A chuckle hovers behind my lips as I pass the people browsing the shelves, sitting in chairs, sipping on over-priced drinks ...

Stupid prey. They have no idea there's a predator amongst them.

Is The Divide down? No. Do I give a flying fuck? Also, no. It eats through my magic, but with it being so close to the summer solstice, I'm powerful enough to push through and hold myself here.

My kind, the nepha, have always been one of the few species able to cross The Divide close to or during a time of power—winter and summer solstice, vernal and autumnal equinox, all hallow's eve, and a few others.

I haven't found the source of the unease from yesterday, but a different thread of magic has drawn me to this shop. It continues to pull me towards the back of the store until I round a floor-to-ceiling bookcase. A small reading nook greets me. It's enclosed by two walls painted a deep blue and two "walls" made of bookshelves. Thick rugs blanket the creaky wood floor, and I step over one of the many large pillows scattered about. As I sink into one of the four overstuffed chairs, I cross my legs and wait for the only other person in this little space to acknowledge me.

Resting my chin on my hand, I read the spines of some of the books. I'll wait for her to speak first. This is a power play—everything is between monsters. I'm patient enough to win. That's how I've risen to the top.

But oh, how lonely it is all the way up here. No, not lonely. I'm not lonely. I'm bored.

And that's why I'm here. There's something going on in this town, and I want to know what. A little mystery to solve, something to pull me from my deepening apathy.

The little chandelier overhead casts broken light from its stained glass. A poor fixture to read by, but the addition of adjustable lamps curved over each chair makes up for it.

The way the fractured light of the pendent spills over

the white-blond hair of the woman reading in the chair opposite me makes her look like a Picasso painting.

I conjure a steaming cup of tea, the scent of apples and cinnamon wafting from the porcelain cup as I take a sip.

With a sigh, she closes her book with a soft thud. She uncrosses and re-crosses her long legs, her skirt flowing around her ankles. Setting the book on a side table, she taps her pointed nail on the arm of her chair. I smirk as that nail lengthens into a claw. I know she means it as a threat, but I only find it amusing that she'd try.

She tsks, drawing my gaze to her angelic face as she asks, "What brings the great Malicious to the human realm?"

"Hello, it's nice to see you too, Galathiel." My eyes flick to the Bible shelved in the middle of the bookcase behind her. With a flick of my power, the book tumbles to the floor, the thin, gold-foiled pages flopping open. "Or should I call you, Gabriel?"

She rolls her eyes. "I don't do that anymore." When I raise a brow, she sighs. "Not that often. You used to do it too, *Archangel Michael*."

It's a struggle to keep my chuckle contained. Ah, the glory days of appearing in the sky over a battlefield. Sometimes I wore my actual form, other times I'd add eyes, arms, extra wings ... I'd often hover over a battle, wings flapping to reflect the sunlight just right. I never knew nor cared what the humans were fighting over, but more often than not, "god" was screamed in one language or another as they stabbed, sliced, beat, and trampled each other. Then later came the guns and bombs.

Humans are clever. I find them interesting. The multitude of ways they've come up with to kill each other is impressive. Humans are complicated, fascinating creatures.

I rub my hand over my lips to hide my smile from Galathiel as I recall how I used to just pick a side, tell them "god" was with them, then I'd "smite" their enemies. So many bodies, so many souls.

The humans started calling us angels, and our power only grew with each human soul consumed. We glutted ourselves, easily rising to the top of the monster hierarchy.

Ancients are the only ones with more power.

I'm pulled from my thoughts as Galathiel's nails tap the wood surface of the small table to her right. A guarded expression makes her beautiful face seem frozen, her flat gaze holding mine as she asks, "Seriously, Malicious, why waste the magic to be here?"

I shrug, not about to share my suspicions. "I could ask you the same."

Her eyes flick towards the main room beyond this little nook before she drops her gaze and shrugs. "It's something to do."

I understand that sentiment all too well. "Same. I just felt like getting out of the house."

She snorts, re-crossing her legs again. "You mean that hideous castle you call home?"

I press my hand to my chest in feigned offense. "Hideous? I'll have you know it's known as the treasure of the mountain pass."

"Yeah, by you."

I smile, leaning forward slightly. I hold her gaze. Her eyes flash a luminous silver before turning back to a cold, ice blue. Parting her lips, her gaze travels down my body like she's picturing me without my clothes. I'm sure she's successful, and not just because most of our kind don't bother with clothing unless we're mingling

18

with the gullible humans. Galathiel and I have known each other ... intimately. But that was a long, long time ago.

When I remain silent, my mocking smile firmly in place, she shifts in her chair, and I can practically feel her anxiety rising. Wicked intent fills my eyes, and she sinks deeper into the cushions as I say, "So you're breaking your boredom by coming here to ... *read*." I push my magic into the small space around us. Her shiver of fear makes my toes curl.

She glances towards the main part of the shop again before dropping her gaze, her nails nearly punching holes in the arms of her chair. "Are you claiming this territory? I heard the dremar, Paine, laid claim here to protect his mate."

Again, her eyes flick over my shoulder.

Interesting. What has her so interested in *this* particular place?

With a slow inhale, I take another sip of my tea before vanishing it with my magic

I sit back and cross my ankle over my knee, grinning. "Yes. I am."

Her head stays bowed, but her hands clench and she grits her teeth before she disappears.

Hmm. Very interesting. Galathiel is up to something. Is it the same thing I'm here for? Tilting my head back, my eyes unfocus on the stained-glass fixture above me. What is it about this location in the human realm? Fated mates are rare enough, but to be mated with a human ...?

I've searched for so long. I'm so lone—

No! I'm just bored. Mind numbingly, eternally bored.

Something is going on in this seemingly inconsequential town where not one, but two human mates have been found. First, Paine, the dremar found his human woman.

Just like the humans call my kind angels, they call Paine's kind gargoyles, and well ... close enough.

Then, the little poisonous anza, Vex, found their human male.

Both monster's mates just *happen* to live on the same street in this town.

I rise from the chair to leave, and a female voice brings me out of my thoughts. "This is my favorite shop. Great coffee. Good selection of books, and they are always happy to order anything for you if they don't have it."

I step out of the reading nook only to have a little human female bounce off my chest. She stumbles back, hitting a bookcase. Her eyes widen as she looks at me, and ... something familiar tickles my brain. That same sensation from yesterday. Before I can delve deeper into the sensation, another woman at her side exclaims, "Oh! Are you okay?"

I can't peel my gaze from the small female who ran into me. Her dark hair is shaved on the sides, the longer velvety strands on top falling over her emerald eyes as she ducks her face. Her tank top shows off toned, tanned arms leading to delicate fingers. Despite her small size, her legs seem to go on forever, revealed by her short shorts.

Fuck. She's delicious.

She pushes off the bookcase she fell against with a nervous smile, and her voice caresses me like a hug as she says to the other woman, "I'm fine. I'm not normally this clumsy, I swear."

The other woman chuckles as the pixie-like female lifts her eyes to me. "Are you okay?"

Both women face me, and I cross my arms. "No harm done."

From the corner of my eye, I see the other woman cross her arms, mirroring me like I'm not the most powerful being she's ever been in contact with. How do humans have so little ingrained self-preservation?

The woman who ran into me does look slightly ... spooked. She darts her gaze around before visibly calming herself with a deep breath. Is there something else besides me that scared this little creature?

The other woman snorts. "You shouldn't apologize, Summer. *He* ran into you."

Summer. Summer. Summer.

The name floats and dances in my mind.

Summer's face loses some of the tension it was holding, and the prettiest smile lifts her cheeks. "I think it was a mutual running-into."

I smile back at her. "A fated collision, if you will."

She blinks at me, and I wonder at my own choice of words. Summer's eyes focus over my shoulder, her expression turning startled, then she looks at the other woman, who just looks mildly annoyed. Summer turns back to me, her eyes tracing over my body before she drops her gaze with a little shake of her head.

I have no idea what's going through her mind, but before I'm able to come up with something else to say to hear her voice again, my attention snaps behind the two women.

Magic punches into me, but I don't budge, not even an inch. What appears to be a human man comes around a corner, the two drinks in his hands vanishing with a pulse of power. I'm reaching for Summer before I can think about it, but the man comes up behind the other one, wrapping an arm around her chest, pulling her against him with a possessive growl. Ah. So, this is Paine's mate. I was so focused on Summer, I didn't recognize her. And honestly, I probably wouldn't have recognized her anyway. I don't concern myself with the particulars of humans ... usually.

But my heart definitely sunk into my stomach when I thought Paine was coming for Summer.

Without his blue skin, horns, wings, and tail, Paine looks, well, painfully human. But his magic is rolling off him in an obvious warning. The mate bond must dull one's self-preservation, because even though this dremar is powerful, very powerful, he's nothing compared to me. And despite knowing this, he's still threatening me.

Though, I guess if I had my own mate, I'd do anything for them. My eyes drift to Summer. I'd hunt down the last glimmer of light from the farthest star for my mate.

With his eyes on me, Paine leans down, whispering in his female's ear. I hear the word nepha, and I sneer as her eyes go wide before she schools her features. Fate has gifted Paine a brave mate. She grabs Summer's hand, pulling her towards the exit ... away from me. I have the sudden urge to seal every door and window in this book shop to keep Summer from escaping.

With great effort, I pull my attention away from the retreating women as Paine crowds my space. I give him some grace, not immediately draining his magic at his impudence. Cocking a brow at him, I nod over his shoulder. "Congratulations on finding your mate."

He blinks at me before crossing his arms. "This is my territory, Malicious. Go hunt somewhere else."

I pat his cheek like he's a child, and to his credit, he doesn't flinch. "It *was* your territory. It's mine now."

The intentional sting of my magic makes his face twitch, and when I drop my arm, he gives in and takes a step back. "Why? Why here? It's a big planet. Find somewhere else. I won't let you endanger my mate."

Why here indeed?

I shift my weight, cocking my hip. "Are you willing to fight for this territory? You and your mate could move somewhere else. In fact, that is exactly what you should do. As you said, it's a big planet."

Paine shakes his head. "Mira's home is here. Her job. Her life."

The fact that Paine doesn't want to take his mate and run even though he should, supports my theory that there's something about this place. This town. I smile to myself. I'm definitely not bored. In fact, this mystery is turning out to be quite fun.

Looking at Paine, something deep in my chest aches.

Mate. To have a bond that deep, a love so perfectly matched ...

Shifting, I turn and head back into the cozy reading nook. Paine follows me without a word. I don't sit, but turn to face the dremar, crossing my arms. My magic surrounds us, making us invisible while keeping humans away so we can have a private discussion.

"Okay, dremar, I have a proposition for you."

His lips curl at the insult of me calling him by his species and not his name. "Go on then, *nepha*."

I raise a brow with a malicious smile. "I will concede that I've encroached on what *used* to be your territory. And I'm sure your mate bond is driving you hard right now—all those animalistic protective instincts telling you to take me out, even knowing how outmatched you are." Paine growls but dips his head in the slightest show of submission. "Unfortunately, if you do stay here, you'll have to figure out how to reign in that gnawing instinct. Going against me will lead to your death. Then where will your pretty mate be?"

His magic shimmers, his wings flaring wide, his horns spiraling from his head, his tail whipping out. A second later, he gets himself back under control, fixing his human appearance. I chuckle, enjoying his struggle, but before I push him too far, I hold up a hand. "I will offer you payment for the territory."

Paine stares at me for a solid minute, no doubt trying to figure out the catch. Finally, he asks, "Payment?"

"Mmm. I'm feeling generous, so I'll allow you as well as Vex to remain."

Paine tries to hide his shock, but I catch it before he smooths his features and crosses his arms again. "And?"

I laugh at his audacity, but I must admit, I'm enjoying myself, and that's fucking fantastic. "And"—I hold out my hand—"I'll give you a three-second hit of my magic every, let's say, every four months or until I lose interest and move on."

His eyes dip to my hand before coming back to my face. "Every week."

"Three months."

"Once a month. And Vex gets a hit too."

Interesting. Are the mated pair working together? Are they ... friends?

Fascinating.

"But if I ever call you, no matter when or for what, you will come."

Paine waits a beat before nodding.

I nod back, holding out my arm. "Deal."

Paine clasps his hand around my forearm. I release my magic, letting him pull it inside himself for the count of three. I assumed I'd have to rip my arm from his grip, but as soon as the three seconds are up, Paine releases me. He rolls his shoulders with a shudder.

Yes, I know. He certainly got the better end of this deal. But not if I find what I want. What I've wanted for so, so long. My someone. My only one.

Paine turns to leave, and I drop the magic shield around us. Before he steps out of the nook, he looks over his shoulder at me. "Why? Why here? Why now?"

I shrug with a smirk. "Why not? It seems to have worked out for you and Vex."

Paine looks me up and down, and I know I've said too much, but he doesn't say anything. He turns and leaves, but I swear I catch his lips twitching with the beginnings of a smile.

As soon as the dremar's magical presence fades, my thoughts shift. I'm intrigued. I'm ... entertained. I hadn't really thought it through, but I think I'll set up what the humans call a base of operations. I won't stay in the human realm all the time; I won't drain my magic unnecessarily, but being here will make it easier to investigate, and maybe find ...

Summer's green eyes flash through my mind.

I shake off the memory of the tempting female.

I clench my hands in frustration. My power continues to syphon away as I fight The Divide to stay in the human realm, yet Paine and Vex can stay here all the time if they wish at no cost to their magic.

It's a well-guarded secret that the strength of a true mate bond snaps the magic of the veil of The Divide that keeps monsters and humans separated. Not many monsters know this, but I've done my research.

I roll my shoulders, once again missing the weight of my wings. What type of dwelling should I go with this time? Maybe something modern. A small house, open and spacious. To avoid prying eyes, I'll wait for The Divide to fall tonight. While the humans are all locked behind their precious blood-carvings, I'll use my magic to construct a house nearby—close enough to keep an eye on things, but far enough to give Paine, Vex, and their mates the perception of space.

In contrast with my other homes, I think this time I'll create something with stark white walls where I can showcase some art. Picasso jumps to mind, but then, Summer's face flashes through my thoughts, and Picasso seems wrong. No. I need Vangogh's *Vase with Twelve Sunflowers*. I need his *A Meadow in The Mountains*. I need Renoir's *Bal du moulin de la Galette*. And on second thought, I will add a Picasso. His *Two Women Running on a Beach*.

And just for fun, in my bedroom, I'll add Raphael's piece, *St. Michael Vanquishing Satan*. The archangel in the famous painting doesn't look all that much like me, but I find it amusing.

I laugh as I step outside, and the sun warms my human skin. How I long to unfurl my wings and let my black-tipped bronze feathers glint in the light. We don't have a sun in our realm, and I've always found our world of perpetual night darkly beautiful. But now, something about the summer sun makes me want to take to the skies and dance through the puffy clouds.

CHAPTER 4

SUMMER

Today was ... fun. Pancakes and books. Pretty close to perfection.

I wasn't sure if I'd be able to relax around strangers, not after ... everything, but Mira made liking her easy, and I think I can safely say I have a new friend.

I smile as I turn out the lights and scooch down into the soft blankets, settling into the king size bed. So much space. I could sleep sideways and still have room to spare.

A girl could really be thrown around on this mattress.

The man from the bookstore this morning pops into my mind. I clench my thighs as a pulse of liquid heat throbs between my legs. He was ... intimidating, but oh so yummy. He was tall, with a built body that wasn't too muscular like some of the people you see at the gym lifting absurd amounts of weight. No, his build was ... how can I describe it? A practical strength. Like whatever he does day to day has built his physique.

And his eyes. The throbbing between my thighs grows more insistent. They were a grey that turned silver depending on the angle. He was ... I wish Mira hadn't dragged me from the store. I nearly dug my heels in as we exited into the late afternoon summer heat. I tried and failed to come up with an excuse to go back in. I wanted bookstore man's name. I wanted to experience that flutter in my chest again when he looked at me. I wanted ...

The blue light from the screen of my phone snaps me out of my thoughts, all the sexual buildup draining away in an instant. I hate that my fingers tremble as I reach for my phone. I have to be stronger than this. He can't win. I won't let him.

I sigh with relief when the preview bubble pops up on my lock screen. It's just an email from the townhouse rental company to make sure I'm settling in okay. I open my new email app, reading through the message. I don't bother with a reply since one isn't needed, and I delete it.

I've turned off all my other notifications, so there are no little red dots to tell me how many likes and comments I have waiting for me. Like the addict I am, my heart rate speeds up as my finger hovers over one of my social media app icons.

I've made a name for myself. I make good money, and I like what I do. I've received plenty of troll comments and messages telling me that being an "influencer" is a young person's game, but at thirty-six, I like to think my maturity and life experience helps lend weight to my curated content. It's a lot of work coming up with and executing what I hope are engaging and informative posts, but to actually get paid for doing something I love ... it's the dream, right?

I thought so. No, it is. I enjoy my work. I did until him. All it takes is one asshole ...

Instead of opening any of my socials, I go back to my new email app and bring up the message chain from the man I hired to help me. I scroll past the introduction message and past the application letter. Slowing down at the welcome email with its attachments, I open the one I'm looking for. I've read it several times, but it's become something like a meditation for me. It makes me feel more in control when I can mentally check off items he recommended I do.

I got a new phone and number and purchased an additional burner number from one of the services he listed. This way, I never have to use my actual number online. Check.

I've deleted all my email accounts and set up three new ones through one of the services he recommended. Check.

When I read over the next line item, I frown. I couldn't delete all my social media accounts. They are my livelihood. I've worked hard to build my little empire. I can't just start over, but I did get rid of one that I wasn't using all that much anyway. And to be honest, it felt good hitting the delete account button. Check.

I followed his advice on how to better secure the accounts I've kept, making sure to turn on every setting that gives me the best possible privacy. Check.

While I have my phone open, I double check the new security apps I've downloaded, including the VPN. Check.

Opening his latest email to me, some of the tension drains from my bunched shoulders. It's good to know I have someone on my side, even if it's someone I've only communicated with via email. This last message suggested I take a break, that I cross-post to my socials to let my followers know I'd be unplugging for a while. Check.

The email is simply signed, Max, with his company

slogan under his name ... *Here to help protect your biggest asset - your identity.*

I close the email, dropping my hand in my lap.

My identity.

I've put so much of myself out there. I believe that being genuine and sincere is the only way to really make a connection over the internet. I've prided myself on being authentic, but with everything that's happened, I realize I've kept very little of myself just for me. I left myself open for this kind of thing to happen.

I don't blame myself, though. Yes, I should have been more careful, but no matter what, no one has the right to do what that creep has done. *He's* in the wrong. Not me.

I stare at the dark screen of my phone in my lap, my grip tightening.

It started innocently enough with a few comments on my posts on one of my social media accounts. No big deal. Comments are great for engagement. But then he began commenting on every single post. And if I didn't respond, he'd comment again, and again, and again. Then he found all my other accounts, commenting on everything and sending me DM's.

It was so frequent, I began to feel uneasy, so I started ignoring him. That only made it worse. Pictures started coming with the messages and DMs; a styled plate of food at a fancy restaurant, a sunset, a painting at a gallery ... with comments like how he'd love to take me to this restaurant, how the sunsets would be that much more beautiful if I was there with him ...

Then he sent me a picture of himself, from the neck down, with the comment, "Do you like this outfit? I think it goes well with that dress you wore last week."

I blocked him so fast, my fingers couldn't move any quicker. But the next day, he was there again under a new account name. Over and over I blocked and reported, but he kept showing up.

And then I got an email. Luckily, it was close enough to one of his social account names that I recognized it before opening it, and blocked and deleted it. It was frustrating and a little nerve-wracking, but honestly, this kind of thing happened every so often.

But a couple of weeks ago, I realized I might be in actual danger. I was leaving the grocery store when my phone buzzed. As I opened the text, my bags fell to the ground. I nearly vomited there on the sidewalk. It was a picture of me in the grocery store from just a few minutes prior. In the image, I had my basket slung over one arm, and I was holding a bunch of bananas in the other. The text read, "I like that you are taking care of yourself and eating healthy. Such a good girl for me."

I deleted the message and turned off my phone. I *never* turn off my phone—at least I didn't use to. I was so disgusted; I was shaking with fear. That man was in the store with me. He took my picture, and he somehow had my number.

That night, I didn't sleep. Instead, I spent hours getting angrier and angrier. Despite my rage, I jumped at every little noise as I talked to the authorities, who did absolutely nothing. In my country, to get a restraining order, I'd need to provide evidence of the existence of violence or serious threat. Which I didn't. All I had were the messages my stalker sent me, and a bunch of his social media account names, half of which were no longer being used. I didn't even know what he looked like since any pictures he sent of himself were cropped so his face wasn't showing.

I'd never felt more alone.

All night, I played the 'what I should have done

game.' I should have run back into that grocery store and found him. To do what? Punch him in the face? Throw a watermelon at him? Cause a scene? Slap him? Kick him in the balls? Something.

But I fled. And while that was probably the right answer, I still play out fantasies of swinging my grocery basket into the side of his face, then standing over his laid-out body, my foot pressed to his throat.

But I'm not that brave. Obviously. My fight or flight apparently leans heavily to the flight side.

Early the next morning before The Divide fell for the day, I was on my way to check my mailbox when I noticed a letter stuffed in my door. With shaking fingers, I opened the folded paper. Tears blurred the words, and I had to blink a few times to read the note that said, *You shouldn't push yourself so hard. You didn't sleep at all last night. You need your rest.*

I stood there, resisting the need to slam the door and hide inside. Instead, I forced myself to look around. It was so early, none of my neighbors were out. Soft birdsong floated on the breeze, and the golden light of the impending sunrise would have been beautiful if it wasn't tinged with my fear. And outrage.

There was no movement, but to my imagination, I was sure every shadow hid my stalker. I could feel him watching me, and it made my skin crawl.

I crumpled the letter, ready to throw it out as I stormed inside my house, slamming the door behind me. I wanted to burn it, but I flattened it out, putting it in a file as evidence.

After that, the deliveries began. Two, three, four times a day. Flowers, takeout from my favorite restaurants, lingerie ... One afternoon, everything off my Amazon wishlist showed up. Every single thing. The note read, *Your wish is my command.*

I refused delivery and canceled my account. And yes, looking back, I know I should have reached my limit before that point, but I was finally angry enough, and scared enough, and tired enough. I was done. I needed help.

I went on a deep dive on the internet. That's where I found Max and his identity protection services. After our initial email, I confessed I didn't feel safe in my home, and he immediately sent me drafted proposals from several security companies in my area. I had cameras in and around my house the very next day. That's also when Max recommended I take a vacation, literally as well as from social media. He said it would be good for my mental health, which I agreed with. He also promised to dig into my stalker's identity.

So, here I am.

Why *here*? I'm not sure. When Mira asked why I didn't pick a more touristy place, I fumbled for an answer, because honestly, I just sort of ended up here. I wanted to leave all that fear and anger behind, if only for a little while. I could afford to travel, so I did, purchasing the soonest available airline ticket I could find. Once at my destination, I purchased another ticket right there in the airport. Upon landing, I bought another ticket to ... I don't even remember where. I told myself this was the only way to fight back—to remove myself from my stalker's proximity. I was like a bartender, cutting my stalker off.

He'd had enough of me, and I wasn't going to give him any more.

And so, I didn't stop.

My mind was spinning darker and darker scenarios. I told myself I was being irrational, but I was sure he was still following me, and because I didn't know what his face looked like, he could have been anyone in any of the several airports I went through. My imagination was in overdrive.

I took three more flights, staying in airport hotels while The Divide was down, until I was too tired to keep going. Using an internet cafe at the airport in Quebec, I found this townhouse rental in the States. It's comfortable and though it shares two walls with the neighbors, it's quiet. I like being sandwiched in. It's morbid, but at least I know someone will hear me if I scream.

Thinking about my house back home, I realize I don't want to go back. The thought of returning makes that echoing loneliness spread through my chest. But my life is there, and I just spent a small fortune to have that security system installed. Though I can always have the cameras shipped here, or somewhere, anywhere. I *hate* how scared I am to return home, but even more, I hate the idea of my stalker winning, of him chasing me away.

I shake my head, easing my grip on my phone as I say to myself, "Let's not get ahead of ourselves, Summer. Let's wait and see what Max finds. Maybe there will be something he can dig up on my stalker that will help me get a restraining order or something. Forget about that loser. Enjoy your vacation."

With that thought verbalized, I reopen my phone and tap on my new messaging app. Reaching for the napkin on the bedside table, I type in Mira's number and send her a quick text.

> "Hi. It's Summer. Sorry. I know it's late. It was so nice meeting you, and I hope we can get together again soon. I'm here for a few weeks, and I'd love for you to show me around if you have the time."

A second later, the little three-dots bubble pops up, and her reply comes through.

> "Text me whenever. I silence my phone when I go to bed, so you don't have to worry about waking me up. I had a great time as well. I'd love to show you around! I'll come up with a few things you might like. I'll text you tomorrow after I get off work around noon."

I type a reply with a smile.

> "Sounds good. And thanks."

She 'hearts' my message, and I close the app before turning off my phone. It's not as much of a struggle as it was at first to watch the screen go dark. Do I want to check on my socials? Hell yes. It's like an itch deep in my brain.

Instead, I lay back, pulling the covers to my chin. Closing my eyes, I start my nightly meditation, but find my thoughts wandering more than usual. It's not worries over my business, or fearful thoughts about my stalker. No, my mind keeps conjuring the man from the bookstore. I do my best to acknowledge my thoughts and go back to my breathing, but my brain won't let him go. My meditation turns into a game of striptease, and with every slow exhale, I peel away a piece of his clothing.

I fall into a vivid dream/meditative state where I find myself pressed against a bookshelf in the back room of that bookstore. His giant bronze wings that I swear I saw in the bookstore flare wide, blocking out the rest of the world. My legs are wrapped around his waist, and his lips kiss and taste my collarbone, my neck, my ear. I groan, not sure if the sound actually came from my lips or if it was just in my dream, but suddenly, I'm naked, and so is he. He grinds his cock between us, and molten fire pools in my belly. He leans forward, his words eliciting a shiver of excitement as he whispers, "You are mine, Summer." His cock lines up with my soaked entrance, and my head falls back, anticipation screaming through me.

He grunts my name as he thrusts into me, the force driving me painfully against the shelves. A book tumbles to the floor with a loud thud, and I snap awake. Sitting up, I grip my sleep shirt over my chest, feeling my racing heart against my fist. I pat my lap, realizing my phone is gone. Leaning over, I see it where it fell to the floor. That must have been what woke me.

Damn it. And just when it was getting good. And why, oh why, didn't I think to bring my vibrator?

I finally get my heart to slow down when the first warning siren goes off outside. I startle, pulling the blankets tighter around my body. Just a few more minutes until The Divide falls.

Last night on my first night here, I was sure I'd be kept up with the sounds of monsters growling and screeching outside, but there was none of that. I wonder if it'll be just as quiet tonight. I have the urge to leap out of bed and double check all the thresholds and sills. Maybe I should add a little more of my blood to the carvings?

I tsk at myself, settling back into the fluffy blankets as the second siren goes off outside, the automated voice saying, "One minute until The Divide breach." Shifting to my side, I close my eyes, but a few seconds later, they pop open. I kick off the blankets with a huff and stand, saying to myself, "You're being ridiculous, Summer."

Still, I make my way around the house with my little safety pin in hand. The final siren blares. I prick my finger, letting a few drops of red blood plop to each engraved windowsill and threshold. For a moment, it feels like I'm being watched. My skin prickles and the little hairs on the back of my neck stand up. The sensation goes away as quickly as it came.

To calm myself, I make a cup of herbal tea. The scent of peaches and green tea wafts around me as I head back to bed. It remains quiet as I wrap a band-aid around my finger. I take a few sips of the tea before setting it on the stone coaster on the bedside table. I'm sure I'm too wound up to sleep, but I force my eyes closed and count my breaths.

CHAPTER 5

MALICIOUS

My head whips around. There it is again. That itch, that tingling down my spine, that awareness of ... *something*. It feels like ... like magic, but old magic. Really old. I send my power into the night, searching. I get little tastes, little licks of sensation, but I can't seem to lock on to it. After a few minutes, my magic loses the trail, so I pull it back to me just as The Divide falls.

Without having to concentrate on keeping myself on the human side of the veil, I'm easily able to direct my magic to the grassy stretch of land before me. I coax the elements to come together, the idea in my head materializing into a physical house with a view of the man-made lake with the pretty park on the far side. I'm less than five miles from the street where Paine lives, but it feels like another world here. More green space. More room. More privacy.

I layer my magic into the house, creating the memory that it's been under construction for several months. I can't have humans coming around to gawk at the house that popped up overnight.

I dematerialize my clothing as I walk through the entrance. I've never cared for clothes, and I don't wear them unless I'm trying to pass as human. All nepha are beautiful. We are described as angelic for a reason, and I'm no exception. I like to flaunt my ethereal physique. My only adornment settles on my head, a delicate bronze laurel wreath crown.

The shaker-style wood front doors appear, and I smile as my magic creates a perfect replica of Rene' Burri's *Stable and Pool* to hang in the small entryway. I marvel at its beauty. I've always believed human souls are so powerful because they have the capacity to create such wonderful things.

Unlike so many of my fellow monsters, I like humans. Well, maybe not *like*, but I find them fascinating. I enjoy their spirit, creativity, and perseverance. I appreciate their violence and their capacity to love and destroy. Their brief life spans are like a lightning strike—brilliant, loud, and beautiful.

The house is nearly complete as I stride down the galley-style hall, past a small library. At the last second, I add a kitchen. Feeding Summer something I make with my hands would feed something in me.

I smile, my cock growing hard at the thought of the beautiful human woman in my new house—in any of my homes. As I walk towards the single bedroom, I admire the sleek and clean-lined design. It's so unlike my gothic castle in the monster realm, but that's what I like about it. I enjoy both styles equally, as well as my country manor in the valley beyond my castle. At first, when I constructed the modest manor, I worried it was too close to the mountain where one of the last of the four ancients lives. But there was no warning earthquake or bolt of lightning, so I figured I was okay.

I press my hand to the bedroom door, but freeze. Anger spikes my heart rate as I stomp back down the hall. As soon as I enter my kitchen, I drop my voice to a menacing tone. "Enjoy this uninvited visit, Galathiel. It will be your last."

The beautiful nepha turns, her naked, silver skin shimmering. She holds my gaze for a second too long, so I growl at her. She lowers her head as she says, "When you said you claimed this territory, I didn't realize you meant you would be staying in the human realm. Such a waste of magic."

"You needn't concern yourself with what I do or do not do with my territory."

Galathiel raises her head, avoiding my eyes to look around my new house as she says, "It's surprisingly modern, Mal."

"You presume too much familiarity, Galathiel. Get out."

She comes around the island. Her eyes flick to the top of my head, and her lips quirk in a smile. "I like that you're still wearing the crown. Sets off your eyes."

I cross my arms, and her gaze drops to my cock. She takes another step towards me but jerks as I slam my magic into her, keeping her from getting any closer. Her lips pout, and her voice turns seductive. I can't believe tricks like that used to work on me.

She purrs, "Want to christen the place?"

Fury erupts through me, a little voice in the back of my mind raging that this house is for Summer. My power blasts into Galathiel, and her eyes go round as I lift her off her feet, then slam her onto her back. She grunts, her breath punching out of her in a cough. Galathiel recovers after a few breaths, painting a sneer onto her face, but the scrape of her silver metallic wings scrambling against the floor gives away her internal panic.

Stupidly, she laughs. "Oh, come on, Mal. It'll be just like old times. We were good together. I can help you hold this territory."

Like I need her help.

I stand over her, spreading my wings, my eyes flashing with my magic. The fake sneer falls from her lips, replaced by anger. "Seriously, Mal? If this is just boredom, you know how *creative* I can be." When I don't respond, her mouth drops open. "No. Is *that* why you're here? You think because a couple of little monsters found their fated one amongst the humans, that you ...?" When I don't answer—because she is too close to the truth—she cackles, her flawless body arching off the floor. "Oh, Mal. Poor, Mal. How *desperate* you mus—"

I kneel between her spread legs, and she licks her lips. When I reach for her, she pushes her body towards my hand. Instead of cupping the inviting breast she offers, I grab one of her feathers and rip it out.

She screams, though I know it didn't hurt that bad. I twirl her silver feather between my fingers, letting my malicious intent shine through my eyes. She stills, finally realizing the trouble she's in. My magic holds her down, but not so tightly that she can't struggle. I like the struggle. I trace her feather down the front of her body from her collarbone to her pelvis. She hisses in pain as a thin line of silver blood wells up.

I take a guess, and say, "You want to help me hold this territory? Or do you want to keep me distracted so I won't take notice of that pretty woman who was working at the bookstore?"

Galathiel's skin goes white, and genuine fear fills her

eyes. Seems I was right. Maybe it's just a passing amusement, but what if ...

Seriously, what the ever-loving fuck is going on in this town?

I decide to push Galathiel just to see her reaction. I say, "She was quite lovely, and I sensed her soul was potent. She'd be a satisfying meal."

I'm rewarded with a growl as Galathiel snaps at me. "You leave Lilith alone!"

She snaps her lips shut, turning her gaze away from me, realizing she made a mistake. I grin, twirling the point of her feather into the skin of her stomach. "Lilith, huh?"

"Fuck you, *Mal.*"

I get right in her face as my magic coalesces at my chest. A growing pinpoint of light illuminates the horror in her eyes. My voice is eerily calm as I say, "It seems, Galathiel, that you have forgotten your place."

My body gets hotter as my magic increases. Galathiel whimpers, "Please, Malicious. I'm sorry. Please, don't."

There are few things that can kill a nepha. An ancient certainly can with no problem. But another way to kill one of us is through what the humans call our "holy light." The very light that I have aimed at Galathiel.

She tries to scramble away from me, but my magic has her pinned. Again, she begs, "Please."

I extinguish my light, and she swallows. "Thank you, Malicious. You're right, of course. I'm hungry, that's all. I could use a boost of magic. The woman is nothing. She just caught my eye, and I thought I might have a little fun with her before I consumed her soul."

I raise a brow. Nice try. "But remember, Galathiel, this is now *my* territory. So ..."

Anger, fear, then feigned boredom all march across her face. "You want Lilith? Go ahead."

I stare at her, my lips quirked in a smirk. Galathiel remains silent for five whole seconds before she huffs a breath. "Fine, Malicious. You win. I want her. May I ... please have her?"

I remove the feather from her flesh and lick her silver blood from the tip, savoring the burst of her magic as I consume it and make it mine. Cocking my head, I wait, enjoying making her sweat. I grin, sitting back on my heels. Crushing her feather in my hand, I watch as silver dust sprinkles onto my brand new floor. "Yes, Galathiel, I will grant you this gift, but you will owe me."

When I release her, she sits up, her skin glowing a brighter silver as she heals the long gash slicing down her middle. I rise, spreading my bronze wings, the metallic black tips scraping against my pristine white walls as I command. "Get. Out. If I see you again without my summons, I'll take your wings."

She curls said wings around her body before she disappears. Immediately, I throw up magical wards around my house and the surrounding property. Nothing will be able to get close without me knowing, not a monster, a human, or even a squirrel.

I use my magic to clean up the mess in the kitchen before padding back towards my new bedroom. I open the door, looking at the large king-size bed with its blue velvet bedding. White curtains cover the floor-to-ceiling windows, and a flick of my wrist lights the stained-glass pendant that hangs over the bed. It's the same one that was in that bookstore, only bigger. The bookstore where I met *her*.

Suddenly, all I can see is Summer spread over my bed, and I imagine crawling to her like a supplicant. Her tan thighs would fall open, and I groan as I picture her sweet pussy glistening for me. What would she smell like? Taste like? Feel like?

My cock stands at attention, and I grip it, slicking my pre-cum down my length. My magic surges from me, doing something I've never seen it do before. It creates a writhing form on my bed. It's her. My magic has made me a Summer. She is slightly transparent, but her small body arches off the bed, and I go to her. When I touch her inner thighs, she's solid enough to grip. Pressing her wide, I watch her phantom pussy clench in anticipation. I flatten my palm to her lower belly, slowly tracing my touch up her body. She shivers, her mouth falling open, her throat bobbing. I imagine a moan coming from those lips, and I growl as my cock throbs with need for her.

My hands wrap around her thighs, and I slam into the magical apparition. It's not quite right. S*omething* is missing, something I imagine only the real Summer could give me, but it's enough to have me rutting into my magic. I make the ghost of Summer hold my gaze as I thrust into her over and over. I can see my dick through her skin, and I growl as I go deeper. My magic weighs her down to keep her from shifting up the bed as I drive into her with increasing strength. My legs are shaking. I'm so close, but there's a whisper at the back of my desperate mind telling me it's not really Summer. That this is a poor copy. That the real thing is out there.

I'm going to find her. I'm going to find out what she really feels like taking my cock. I'm going to learn what sounds she makes as she comes. I'm going to memorize every touch that makes her squirm. I'll learn what steals her breath. I'll find out how to make her beg for me.

I'm going to destroy that little human.

My orgasm flashes through me, my cum spilling into the magical body under me. I rock into her, the sparks of my pleasure fading to tingles until I'm spent. Tucking my wings, I roll onto my back, my magic dispersing the fake Summer, cleaning my cum in the process.

I press my hand to my chest over my racing heart. Well, that was ... interesting.

Hours later, The Divide starts to pull at me as the magical veil begins to go back up. I realize I haven't moved from this spot on my bed. I've been staring at the ceiling thinking about ... her.

I slip through The Divide into the monster realm of Ekenys. I've spent enough magic for one day. Spreading my wings, I aim for my castle. Hope skips like a child through my heart. Could Summer be my ...? No. No. After all these centuries, it wouldn't be that easy.

Still, the thought of her ...

I laugh at the stars as I barrel-roll through a cloud. The cool mist clings to my bronze skin, and I shake it off, my laugh getting louder.

I'm certainly not bored anymore.

CHAPTER 6

SUMMER

Happy and content, I sigh as I look around the busy farmer's market. A week has somehow both stretched out languidly and flown by. There has been no word yet from Max, but still I've been able to mostly shut off the worries about my stalker.

I've spent much needed time by myself, working out in the mornings, fixing myself meals, and reading. God, reading. I didn't realize how little time I was leaving myself to enjoy a good book. I've gone through two this week, picturing the man from the bookstore as the main character in each one.

I can't stop thinking about him. I've even dreamed of him, waking wet and needy—to the point I ordered myself a little vibrator. Different from the one I left at home, this one is a simple C-shape that hits my inner walls and my clit perfectly. My fingers were fine, but having that vibration on my clit is next level. With my imagination providing the image of the man from the bookstore doing all sorts of things to me ... well, I've worn myself out a few times.

The buzz of the farmer's market fades as I daydream of bookstore man's black hair and silver eyes. The way he looked at me, like he was trying to figure out a puzzle ... the memory makes me shiver.

Mira laughs, bumping my shoulder with hers. "You should ask that tomato on a date if you're going to fondle it like that."

Looking down, I realize I'm rubbing my fingers over the tomato in my cupped hand. I shake my head with a smile, paying the man behind the table, then dropping the fruit in my bag. Mira loops her arm through mine, pulling me towards where Paine is in line at the pastry tent. The sun comes out from behind a cloud. The bright rays cause my eyes to water, and as I blink them clear, I nearly stumble.

Not again.

Transparent wings flare from Paine's back, and barely-there curling horns spear from his head. I glance down at my sandaled feet, and when I raise my head, Paine looks normal.

Mira squeezes my arm. "You okay?"

I smile, hiding my growing anxiety. "Yeah. I forgot my sunglasses."

We join Paine in line, and I grip my shopping bag to keep from running my hands through my hair. Why do I keep seeing these things? I've caught glimpses of wings, a tail, and horns at least half a dozen times this week. And not just on Paine.

Yesterday, there was a woman exiting the bookstore, and I swore she had beautiful silver wings. And the day before that, when I was taking out my trash, I ended up slamming the lid too hard when I saw a shifting of sparkling shadows. The setting sun of dusk made it hard to see what it was, and then it was gone.

I step forward, Mira and Paine letting me order first. As the woman behind the table bags my loaf of sourdough and my chocolate croissant, I dig cash out of my cross-body. Slipping the pastries into my shopping bag, I step to the side to wait for my new friends.

My mind wanders to earlier in the week when we discovered I was renting the house right across the street from Mira and Paine. Mira and I laughed at the coincidence, but Paine ... he didn't seem thrilled at the coincidence. He had mumbled something, and that mirage of horns appeared on his head for a split second.

I'm pulled from my thoughts as a little girl squeals from behind me, and I turn, quickly stepping out of her way as she runs giggling from her scrambling mother. I watch, chuckling to myself. The girl is cute, but the mom looks frazzled. I'm glad I don't have kids. My desire to remain childless has chased off a surprising number of boyfriends. Kids are great ... from a distance, but if I were to choose to have a dependent, I'd get a dog.

The mom finally catches her little girl, lifting her into her arms, juggling toddler and groceries.

A shiver tingles down my spine.

Behind the mother and daughter, there's a faint outline of bronze wings draping gracefully from a man's back. The feathers are so beautiful, the color like a gilded sunset. The more I stare, the more solid the wings become. The man shifts, drawing my eyes to his black hair. There's something familiar about him. I take a step towards him without thinking about it. As I creep closer, the wings fade and disappear. The man turns just slightly, giving me the barest glimpse of his profile.

Bookstore man?

My flip flops are hard to jog in, but I rush to keep up with him. I lose sight of him as he goes around a large tent, and when I make the turn, he's gone. Damn. Rising on tiptoes, I strain to look over the crowd, but even with the few extra inches, I'm still shorter than everyone except the kids.

A deep disappointment settles in my chest. When I take a deep breath, it shudders like I'm about to cry. My brow crinkles as I try to shake off my melancholy. I attempt to laugh at myself for feeling so down, but I can't seem to manage more than a weak smile.

What the heck? Why is my throat burning with the threat of tears? A compulsion comes over me. I need to see him. Just one more time. I push back to my tiptoes, biting my lip, looking around. Where did he go?

"What are you looking for?"

Paine's deep voice drops me to flat feet, and I spurt out the first lie that comes to mind. "I saw someone with an Irish Wolfhound. I love those dogs. I wanted to ask if I could pet it but lost them in the crowd. Being five-two sucks."

Mira chuckles, reaching up to interlace her fingers with Paine's whose arm is draped around her shoulders. Her strange bracelet catches the sunlight, refracting a rainbow of colors. Paine lifts his chin, easily looking over the crowd for a dog that I made up.

And now I feel guilty.

After a minute, Paine turns back to me. "Sorry. Don't see it."

I shrug. "No biggie."

We stop at the lemonade stand. Mira orders a classic, and I order a limeade. Drinks in hand, we exit the market. It's only a short walk to our row of townhouses, and the plastic cup sweats in my hand as I take leisurely sips of my tart drink with a hint of sweetness. So refreshing on this perfect summer afternoon.

We part ways on the street, and I shift my grocery bag to my shoulder as I wave goodbye to the adorable couple. Paine kisses the top of Mira's head as they go inside their house.

Locking the front door behind me, I pause in the foyer, a smile on my face. Tomorrow is all about me. I plan to spend my entire day reading and snacking up on the rooftop terrace. I'll work on my tan, drink all the water, then maybe finish the day with a margarita. Or two.

After checking my email to see if there is anything new from Max—there isn't—I put away the few dishes I left out to dry this morning. I clean the sink, then turn out the lights as I make my way upstairs. After a long, hot shower, I pull on my sleep shirt and slide into bed. I grab my e-reader and snuggle into my pillow.

I jerk awake, the warning siren pulling me from my dream. I lift my e-reader off my chest where it must have fallen when I fell asleep. Setting it on the side table, I lay back and stare through the darkness at the ceiling. The edges of the dream I was having clings to my mind. There was beautiful bronze light everywhere. And there were wings. So wide, they took up my entire view. I could have spent my whole night dreaming of those wings.

The second warning siren goes off, the automated voice blaring through the streets. "One minute until The Divide breach."

I count down in my head until the final siren goes off, and as it fades, the world around me goes silent. I hold my breath, waiting for the sounds of monsters. Nothing. It's quiet outside. I pull my covers up to my nose, unable to shake the feeling of being watched.

Stalker.

No. I'm not going to think about that right now. Besides, that's impossible. I'm an ocean away, and The Divide is down. I'm safe.

Still, I toss and turn, unable to get comfortable. No matter how many breathing techniques I try, no matter how many stupid sheep I count, I can't seem to fall asleep.

With a huff of frustration, I kick the covers off my body and stomp downstairs. I gulp down a glass of water, but that only seems to wake me more. I could watch tv. Glancing towards the living area, I stand in the center of the room. TV doesn't sound appealing right now. Should I go back upstairs and try to read again?

Back in the kitchen, I open and close drawers and cabinets, the soft banging sounds echoing quietly through the house. I'm not sure what I'm looking for, but I find myself staring into the small pantry, not really seeing the contents. I'm not hungry anyway. But ... I need something to do. It feels like I had an entire pot of coffee. I can practically feel my blood racing through my veins. I've felt this way a few times over the years, but never to this extent. The kitchen almost vibrates around me.

I shake my arms, getting my shoulders involved until my whole body is wiggling, like I'm trying to expel these jitters. I laugh as I shimmy and shake in the middle of the kitchen. I know I must look absurd, but who cares. It's just me, and this is making me feel better.

I'm still wide fucking awake, though.

A glint catches my eye, and I turn to look at the row of kitchen knives hung on a magnetic board secured to the wall. Hmm. Crossing the room, I pluck one and press my thumb to the tip. There's no accompanying sting, and I tsk, talking to the knife. "You are not living up to your potential, sir."

From my earlier perusal, I know there's a sharpener in the third drawer, so I retrieve it and go to work. One after the other, I draw the edges of the blades across the stone slab. It's satisfying to see the knives grow shiny under my attention. I grab the last one. A filet knife. Carefully, I set it against the stone. This type of knife is difficult to sharpen since the blade is so thin and flexible.

As if my thoughts cause my hand to slip, I yelp, looking down. A long line of bright red blood spreads from right below my pointer finger to the base of my palm. Lifting my hand, I realize the cut is really deep. Like, really, really deep. And now that I've noticed, the pain explodes. I grab a towel, pressing it to the wound. The pressure makes it worse, and I hiss, doubling over.

"Shit. Fuck. Son of a bitch!"

I pull the towel away to see it soaked in blood. I'm surprised I can't see bone. Blood drips on the floor, so I lean over the sink. I turn on the water and curse again as my blood gushes down the drain. I can't see how deep it actually is, but I think I'll need stitches.

A heavy thud sounds from outside, and I jump. I hold my breath, listening, and then I hear a snarling growl, a yelp of pain, and a sickening wet crunch. Monsters. Did someone get caught outside or are they fighting each other?

I obviously can't go to the hospital right now. The Divide will be down for several more hours. Recalling I saw a tool kit in one of the cabinets, I wrap the bloody towel tightly around my hand and hunt down the bag I'm looking for. I rummage around before grabbing the little tube, holding it over my head. "Ah ha!"

Okay, now for the hard part. Going back to the sink, I

strip the towel away. Spreading my fingers wide until the cut opens, I squeeze the superglue into my wound.

"Shit. Shit. Shit. Shit." My eyes water, and I grit my teeth as I relax my hand, letting the edges of my sliced skin come together. I add more glue, then drop the tube and use my free hand to pinch the wound closed. I dance in place as pain spears all the way up my arm. It's far from perfect, but as the glue starts to dry, the blood flow slows, then stops.

Looking around, I sigh. "Shit. I should have found bandages or something before doing the glue." I don't want to reopen the cut, so I keep my hand close to my chest, trying to protect it as I move towards the stairs. Hopefully, there are some band-aids in the bathroom ... something to hold me over until I can get to a doctor.

The front door rattles as something large slams into it. I scream, falling against a wall. My hand flexes involuntarily, and hot blood once again spreads over my palm. I don't care about that right now. The windows along the front of the house vibrate with banging thuds, and I'm sure the glass is going to shatter. The curtains are drawn, so I can't see what's out there. I don't know if that's better or worse. When the front door shakes again, I run up the stairs. Glass breaks behind me, but I don't turn. I keep running, slamming the bedroom door behind me. I dash into the bathroom as one of the windows in the bedroom cracks.

What the fuck is happening?

CHAPTER 7

MALICIOUS

It's been a week, and I still can't get Summer out of my mind. I've spent an unwise amount of magic here in the human realm. A few times, I caught a glimpse of her, finding myself frozen in place as I just stared from a distance.

I'm a monster obsessed. I've lost count of the number of times I've used my magic to fuck the magical transparent Summer. Each time I come, sweaty and panting, I swear I've finally gotten her out of my system.

I haven't.

Standing outside my new house, I scent the air, enjoying the night. Stretching my arms wide, I roll my head side-to-side. Maybe I'll go on a hunt. Even if there aren't any humans dumb or careless enough to be out at this hour, there are plenty of monsters I could make a deal with, maim, or kill to replenish some of my magic.

My gaze snaps towards Paine's street. There it is

again. The power washes over me like a concussive wave. Magic. Old magic. The same power I felt a few nights ago, but stronger. The same sensation I felt at the bookstore, but this ... I'm hit with a spine-tingling rush of magic, and ...

MINE.

Delight spears through me as I snap out my wings and take flight. This isn't some feeble trail like before. I'm easily able to follow the hum of power like it's an actual thread lit up in the night sky. I could find the source of this magic with my eyes closed.

As I circle above Paine's street, I'm both unsurprised and frustrated. *Of course* this strange magic is coming from here.

And I'm not the only one who has come for it. Dozens of monsters are already clawing and battering against a townhouse across the street from where Paine and his mate live ... a few doors down from Vex's mate's house. The magic pulsing from inside raises the hairs on my body. *Mine. Mine. Mine.*

In any other circumstance, I would grin at the monsters below tearing at each other to get to the house, only for them to erupt in howling screams as the blood-carvings burn their flesh.

And I can't really blame them. The taste of strong magic dances in the air. But it's floating on the scent of blood, of the blood of my mate. Mine.

I had hoped coming to this place would lead me to the one fated for me. I dreamt of finding my one. But in the back of my mind, I couldn't fully believe, because in all the years of my long, lonely existence, why should fate bless me now?

But there's no denying it now. The tether of magic pulls at me, and I KNOW. My mate is in that house.

I'm stunned. Shocked into stillness, hovering in the air, nostrils flared.

The door to Paine's mate's house flies open, and the dremar bursts out onto the street. Is the pull of this wild magic enough to drag him away from his own mate? He won't get to whomever is in that house. None of these pathetic monsters will be able to get past the blood-carvings. But the magic of the barriers is the least of their worries, for I am here. No one will touch what is mine.

Paine's mate, standing inside her open doorway behind the safety of her carvings, yells out, "Oh, god! Summer!"

The dremar shouts over his shoulder, "The blood carvings will hold, Mira." But still, Paine tears the monsters from the front door and windows, flinging them into the street only to have them claw and scrape their way back. For a long moment, I continue to hover over the scene, my brain slow to put the pieces together.

A window shatters, snapping everything into focus.

The woman from the bookstore. Summer is in that house. Summer is mine.

Fuck. What is it about this place? This town? This street? This can't all be coincidence. Something is going on here, but I leave the mystery for another day.

I dive, slicing the first monster I reach in half with my metal wings. Blood and gore splash against the house but does nothing to deter the other monsters. Burn marks singe their claws from trying to break through the blood-carvings. And I understand. This magic is beyond tempting. Maddeningly so. And it's carried on the scent of blood.

Her blood.

It smells like copper and smoke and the hot summer air before a rainfall. It is intoxicating. It is distracting. I am on the verge of throwing every shred of my magic at the house to get to the woman inside.

Because beyond being my mate, Summer's blood identifies her as a witch—or at the very least, her bloodline comes from a powerful witch family. She has magic. So rare for a human these days. So delicious.

But the smell of blood also means my mate is hurt, and the urge to get to her makes my hands shake. I'm so used to just devouring power from whomever I want without thought. I take without remorse. I don't ... *care*. After living for so long, I can't care about anything but myself. I'm selfish. I'm powerful. I'm bored. A dangerous combination.

But the mere scent of my mate has me feeling ... *feelings*.

It's different. It's exhilarating. I love it.

Paine goes down as an anza tackles him. Vex? No. This anza is female, and more purple than Vex's midnight blue. I harden my skin, ripping the poisonous anza from Paine. I kill three more monsters before a large pack of oulurs come barreling down the street. The humans call these demon-like monsters, oni, with their red or black skin, horns, tusks, and pointed tails. Oulurs will eat anything. The bottom feeders of our world. Vicious and cunning. The thought of these monsters so close to my Summer fills me with a trembling rage.

Paine flies to the roof, chasing off a feathered grae, and from the corner of my eye I catch sight of a silver glimmer in the distance. Galathiel hovers in the air, keeping her distance, but I can see the hunger on her face. She wants Summer's magic too. When she notices me glaring at her, she smartly flies off ... in the direction of the bookstore.

I rip four legs off a menace. The spider-like monster

stumbles on its remaining serrated legs as it scrambles around me back towards Summer's house. I move to intercept it, but I notice Paine's mate. She's wringing her hands from her doorway, leaning too close to her blood-carvings. Even with her right there in sight, the monsters ignore her.

We all want Summer.

One of the oulurs climbs the outside of the building, its long tongue licking its dark red lips.

Enough!

A burst of instinctive, protective hysteria rips through me. My magic gathers in my chest like a tide surge before a great storm. I've lost control.

Shit.

I shout at Paine and catch a glimpse of him flying full speed to his mate's house. He barrels across her threshold a mere fraction of a second before my power explodes out of me in a flash of light. The entire block lights up brighter than the midday sun in this realm. Every monster turns to ash. The street falls silent, but my heart still beats a loud rage-filled rhythm in my ears.

As my light slowly dies, Paine comes back out, and I bark, "Where is Vex?"

Paine's gaze shifts to the townhouse a few doors down from Summer's. "They are in Ekenys. Max, Vex's mate, likes our realm better. They stay at Vex's place most of the time." His eyes travel back to Summer's house. "There aren't many humans left with that kind of power in their blood. I haven't felt something like that in centuries. The fact that she's here, now ..."

I run my fingers through my black hair, the metal points of my crown scraping my hand. "There is something going on here, Paine."

He nods. "I talked to Mira about moving. She doesn't

want to leave any more than I do. But neither of us can really explain why." His leathery wings flutter, and his tail swishes. "You have a theory, Malicious?"

I do, but I'm not ready to share it yet. When I don't answer, Paine sighs. "I'll catch Vex up on what happened." I look around the quiet street before Paine's voice brings my attention back to him as he says, "Something is pulling monsters and their mates to this place. Of all the places Mira could have gone when she moved out of her parent's house in the country, why here? And why was I here in this exact place the night Mira got caught outside after The Divide fell?" He looks up and down the street. "And the fact that of all the anzas I could have caught and brought here last Christmas, I brought Vex ... who *just* happened to find their mate ... who also *just* happens to live on this street.

Too many coincidences. I know Mira would be safer somewhere else, but I ... don't want to leave. I don't know why, and that pisses me off."

Again, I look around. Why, indeed?

Paine lowers his voice, stepping closer. "Is Summer your ...?"

I don't answer. I don't even turn to face him. I simply stare at the shattered window of the townhouse across the street.

Summer.

Paine's voice deepens with concern. "Summer is visiting here from overseas. She traveled a very long way. Malicious, this town is nice enough, but it certainly isn't a vacation destination." He pauses until I turn back to him, my own trepidation rising. "So why did Summer end up here?"

My gaze is pulled back to Summer's townhouse. "I don't know, but I'll find out."

After a long silence, Paine's wings flutter as he turns to go home to his mate. I watch with envy as he tucks his large leathery wings to his back and ducks into this mate's house. She is there on the other side of her open front door, still safely behind her blood-carvings. As soon as Paine steps across, she's in his arms, his hand stroking her back. He closes the door, and I look up and down the street, making sure it's clear.

I'm about to take to the air when a tingle of familiar magic scrapes against my skin. Turning, I scowl at Galathiel. She bows, her silver hair falling around her face.

Still, I snarl. "You must be tired of your wings being attached to your back, Galathiel."

Her shoulders tense as she shakes her head. "Wait, you'll want to hear this." When I don't say anything, she lifts her gaze a fraction, staring at my chest as she says, "I'm giving you this information, but I need your word, Malicious."

"What would you ask of me?"

"Lilith." My lips quirk with the threat of a chuckle, but my mirth fades when she continues, "Lilith is ... mine."

Galathiel's voice cracks, and I tilt my head. "Your mate?"

She nods, curling her silver wings around her body. "I haven't claimed her yet, but when the time is right ..." Her wings fold along her back, the metallic tips scraping the street. "I will not ask her to uproot her life and leave this place. She's mine, Malicious, and I need your word that you will leave her alone. That you'll leave *us* alone."

"And what will you give me in return?"

She jerks her chin towards the street behind me. When I look over my shoulder, I notice a deep scorch mark in the asphalt. Galathiel skirts around me, and I follow her

We stand over the mark, and she points at it. "There. I ended up here two nights ago. I couldn't figure out why. I paced this street for hours, and I realized I kept stopping here, so I marked the spot."

Her bare toe digs into the scorch mark, and I realize she's right. It feels like my magic is pooling in my feet like it's trying to seep into the street. There's something here, and it's incredibly powerful. Galathiel could have taken whatever it is for herself, but she's sacrificing this power to protect her mate.

My gaze stays on the ground as I wave a hand at the silver nepha beside me. "Fine. You and your mate are safe. Go."

I feel her hesitate, but a second later, a gust of wind caresses my skin as she takes off and flies away. My skin feels too tight. I'm literally itching to get to whatever is buried here. The black asphalt begins to crumble as I push my magic into the street. Rock and earth spill out in a widening circle. I back up and keep digging. The power below surges, and my skin starts glowing.

Deeper and deeper.

And then I hit it. My magic brushes against ... something. From the corner of my eye I notice large, branching horns peeking around the corner at the end of the block. A quilen. It doesn't approach, but it stares, licking its lips, its stone-like skin scraping against the brick of a building as it shifts its weight.

I fully expect more monsters to show up. The fact that I just incinerated a dozen monsters doesn't mean shit. The magic buried here would drive any creature to take the risk.

Using my power, I scoop up the palm-sized object,

and as I pull it to the surface, I realize it's a jewel. A black jewel. Wrapping my hand around it, the cold surface burns. I harden my skin, but still the sting makes me wince. The hiss of a snake-like grateslung comes from behind me, so I take off.

I should take this to my castle in Ekenys, but the thought of leaving Summer for even a short time makes me sweat. I lead the monsters away from Summer's street, and with the immense power thrumming off this stone, it's child's play to fling open the doors of my new house. Without slowing, I tuck my wings, flying through the entrance.

Scores of monsters slam against my wards at the edge of my property, but I ignore the growls and screeches. I land in the living room, then quickly stride to my bedroom. As I create an addition to my house, I layer thick magical wards, one over the other. I open the newly constructed hidden entrance and descend. Down, down, down. I keep going until I'm deeper than the original hole where I found this gem. Finally reaching my new safe room, I set the stone on the single pedestal. My magic lines the walls, the floor, and the ceiling of this room.

I stare at the gem. So, this is it. This is what was drawing monsters and their mates to this place. Leaning in, I take a deep breath. It doesn't have a smell. As I circle the pedestal, I realize the bronze light coming from my skin isn't reflecting in the black facets of the stone. I pause, tapping it with an elongated claw. The resulting sound is high-pitched and musical, like a woman's moan at the height of her pleasure. I push my magic towards it but can't penetrate the jewel.

Twenty minutes go by, and I still don't know anything new about this treasure other than that it's pulsing with spine-tingling power. I want it. If I could absorb this magic ... I think I could take on an ancient and survive.

Reluctantly, I leave the jewel behind, securing magical locks behind me as I climb back to my bedroom. There's time to figure out how to crack into the power of the stone, but I need to make sure it's secure.

I layer more of my magic over the hidden door and stand back. My wings shiver as I try to shake off the residual magic of the stone. There's still a faint resonance coming from below, but with all the wards I've placed on the safe room, the stairs, the door, and my entire house, my new prize is as safe as I can make it.

Stepping back outside, I rub my chest. It feels like I'm being pulled in two. I want to stay and keep examining the jewel, but I *need* to get back to my mate.

Summer wins.

I take to the air, grinning at the monsters prowling around my property. I have what everyone wants, and I'm not only referring to the gem. I have found my mate. Excitement sparks through my blood until I'm nearly vibrating.

As soon as I land on her roof, I prowl across her terrace, making sure the area is clear. The ashes of the monsters I killed still float on the hot evening breeze. I look over the short brick wall down at the street, my bronze laurel leaf crown keeping my hair from falling into my eyes. I spend a small burst of magic to fix the giant hole in the street. I also repair the crack in Summer's bedroom window and replace the shattered window downstairs. No task is too small or insignificant for the woman inside this house.

All thoughts of the mysterious jewel fade away. Tilting my head back, I smile at the night sky. Those strange sensations I've been feeling on and off the past few days were Summer. My mate. I can't believe it.

And she's a witch. Does she know?

The scent of her power has almost completely faded, which means she's stopped bleeding. That's good, though I miss it, that smoky taste, that zing of magic. Magic that every monster will want for themselves.

My own magic unfurls, but this time, it's not a violent outpouring of power. It slides from me like honey from a jar, coating the townhouse that holds my little sunshine. My magic seals the building in wards, because even knowing a monster has never gotten past the blood-carvings, they no longer feel like enough when it comes to her.

I want to swoop in and steal Summer away to my castle. Would she struggle? Would she fight me? Would the little human be afraid of me? The thought of playing at fear makes my cock twitch.

With one more sweep of the street below, I spread my wings, and with a strong flap, I leap into the air to patrol my new territory here in the human realm. I have a lot to protect right now.

CHAPTER 8

SUMMER

From the bathtub, the growls and snarls of monsters outside have faded. Something heavy lands on the roof, and I hold my throbbing hand to my chest. I curl my knees to my chest, ducking my head. My entire body trembles as I rock back and forth. "They can't get in. They can't get in. They can't get in."

Around the edges of the closed bathroom door, and the outline of the curtains covering the single window in here, a brilliant bronze light glows. I squint as it gets brighter. The light flashes with an accompanying roar, and I have to close my eyes. I can still see the bronze light behind my eyelids.

I recognize this light. But it can't be. I must be mistaken.

I can feel the light filling every available space. It's warm. I wince as it gets impossibly brighter, and I'm afraid I'll be blinded even with my eyes closed and my face hidden.

Curiosity mingles with my terror. No one survives the light of an angel. I've seen it once, on a video shot on a phone. The clip only lasted seven seconds. It was a view of a city at night from high up, like the person was looking out of a window from the top story of a building. A figure hovered in the distance, wings spread wide, then a flash of silver light exploded on the horizon. A second later, the video went dark.

An angel's holy light.

This light isn't silver. It's bronze. But it's the same. So intense, it's not hard to imagine it purifying the entire world. I want to see. What does an angel look like up close? Are they as beautiful as the rumors suggest? The power of the light surrounding me feels ... hot, tingly, comforting somehow. Like the sting of sunlight but more intense.

Much more intense.

Eventually, the light beyond my closed eyes dims slightly, but the air around me hums with residual power. I'm afraid. Okay, I'm terrified, but ... I ... I want to see. Just a quick look. The angel probably isn't even still there.

As if to prove my thoughts wrong, faint thuds come from the ceiling, like someone or something is walking on the terrace. My heart rate speeds up. Is it up there?

Being careful of my hand, I climb out of the tub. The soft bronze light shimmers like pixie dust around me as it dims. Walking on the balls of my feet, I make my way through the bedroom, into the hall, and quietly tiptoe up the stairs to the terrace. I pause at the door, my fingers trembling slightly as they hover over the handle. I strain to hear if there's still movement out there, but it's quiet.

It's like a scene from a horror movie as I wrap my

hand around the knob and open the door just a crack. I shouldn't be doing this. This is really, really stupid. But I want to know. I want to see. I press my face to the narrow opening, and ...

Holy shit. There's an angel on my roof. His back is facing me. He's ... beautiful. And somehow familiar. And naked, though most of him is concealed by his bronze wings. They drape behind him, the black tips trailing on the floor. His dark hair ruffles in the breeze, a delicate bronze crown circling his head.

I push the door open another few inches, needing to see more, needing to get closer.

The angel spreads his wings, his black hair fluttering in the gust created by the movement. He bends his knees, and I almost call out. With impossible speed, he launches into the air. I stand on my roof, gaping open-mouthed at the starry sky as he disappears.

Damn.

I search the sky for a full minute before I realize what I've done. I'm standing outside in nothing but my over-sized sleep shirt with the sloth on the front ... and The Divide is down.

I sprint to the door, fumbling the handle twice before I wrench it open. Safely on the other side, I press my back to the door, breathing hard. What the fuck was I thinking? Well, I *wasn't* thinking, obviously. It's like I was pulled onto the roof by ... *something.*

Back in bed, I toss and turn, my mind deliciously combining bookshop man and the angel from the roof. Fantasies parade through my imagination until I'm grinding against my vibrator, desperate mewls slipping from my lips as I come once, then twice.

I wish I knew bookstore man's name so I could shout it to the ceiling the next time. I curl my hurt hand, gently running my middle finger along the jagged seam of my cut. It stings slightly, but I don't stop. My mind wanders as I stroke my hand, staring at nothing until my eyes drift closed.

———

I've almost succeeded in shaking off the crazy monster attack from last night. Toweling off my hair from my shower after my workout, I glare at the bedroom window. I could have sworn I heard it crack last night. I tilt my head, tapping my nail to the glass. Nothing. I guess it could have just sounded like it cracked.

Still ...

I hold up my hand, staring at my palm for what must be the thousandth time. This morning when I rolled out of bed, I hadn't noticed the absence of pain until I grabbed my water bottle. When I looked at my skin, there was nothing but a thin white line. The cut had healed overnight.

But how?

Once again, I press my fingers to where the cut was, recalling how deep it was, how painful. But now, there's nothing. In fact, the scar is even more faint than it was earlier this morning. Flexing my fingers wide, I stare amazed. This is so weird.

I shake my head, tying my bikini. Sliding on my terry shorts and a tank top with a sloth doing the upward dog pose, I grab my phone. Before I head to the roof to get my tan on—the roof where I saw an angel—I need to take pictures of the shattered window downstairs to send to the landlord.

On the way downstairs, I check my email. Still nothing from Max. I pause at the bottom of the stairs, setting a three minute alarm. I won't allow myself to get sucked in. Three minutes. Not a second more.

Opening my first social media app, I skim through the ridiculous number of notifications. Happily, most are likes and comments that basically tell me to enjoy my break and to take care of myself. I scroll to make sure I haven't been tagged in anything important from sponsors, then move on to my next account. I'm half-way through those notifications when my alarm goes off. I'm tempted to finish checking, but I close the app and walk into the little library/office at the front of the house.

"Seriously, what the hell is going on?"

Both windows are fine. I speed walk down the hall, checking every window on the first floor. Nothing. I go back to the office and tap on the widows, then rub my hand—my completely healed hand—over the glass.

Am I still asleep? Is this all a dream? What the fuck is going on this morning?

Swinging open the front door, I jog down the steps. Branches scrape my legs as I push through the bushes that line the front of the townhouse. I bend over and pick up a piece of broken glass, muttering to myself. "I knew I wasn't crazy." Looking up, I glare at the perfectly fine window, my middle finger worrying at my healed palm. "Or maybe I am."

"Summer!"

I nearly jump out of my skin as Mira calls out. Working myself free of the bushes, I turn. Mira jogs across the street, and I admit, it's strange not seeing Paine glued to her side. Though I'm sure he's lurking in their house peering at us through the curtains or something. I'd feel uneasy at his possessiveness over her if the two weren't so obviously in love. They are one of those couples that just work, they click, like they were meant to be.

I meet Mira on the sidewalk, and she grips my upper arm, leaning in. "Are you okay? You must be freaked out after last night."

I subtly drop the little piece of glass before stuffing my hands in my pockets. For a second, I consider telling her about the windows and my hand, but I just shrug. "It was a little scary." *Okay, it was terrifying.* "But monsters are part of life. Thank god for the blood-carvings, right?" It's on the tip of my tongue to tell her I saw an angel, but again, I keep it to myself.

She gives me a little squeeze before dropping her hand. "You sure you're okay? Paine and I are going for coffee if you want to come with us."

"Tempting." I point to the rooftop terrace with a smile. "But I have a date with a lounge chair and a good book."

"That sounds heavenly."

"You can join me if you want."

She shakes her head. "Nah. You enjoy your me-time, but maybe we can do a girls day on the terrace next weekend?"

"Perfect."

She walks off with a wave, and I go inside, ignoring the glaringly not-broken window.

Hours later, my skin is wonderfully warm, sweat beading and gathering in my navel. Even though the sun is setting, it's still hot out, and I want to soak up every bit of warmth I can. I've been up here all day with only short breaks to pee, replenish my drink, and grab snacks. And I've managed to only think about bookstore man a dozen times or so.

I sigh, sliding my finger under the string of my bikini bottoms, shifting the fabric to the side. A pale line marks across my skin, showing off my tan. Would bookstore man like my tan lines? Would he lick along that line at my hip?

Damn it. Stop it, Summer.

I pick up my glass, the surface slippery with condensation. I switched from water to margaritas an hour ago, and when I bring the rim to my lips, I find the chili salt gone and the glass empty except for the two slices of jalapeño. I like my margaritas spicy. Was this my third? Fourth?

Doesn't matter. I'm on vacation. Time for a refill.

I smile, swinging my legs over the lounger, flexing my toes against the warm wood floor. Scooping up my towel, slightly damp with my sweat, I head inside and down to the kitchen, my head swimming with a slight buzz.

Okay, I might be drunk.

Opening my favorite playlist, I shimmy and dance as K-pop blares through the house. I grab the big bag of chips and the container of salsa, setting both to the side. The blast of cold air from the fridge sends goosebumps over my skin as I collect the ingredients for my drink. I open every drawer, and hunt behind bottles. Looking at the four limes sitting on the counter, I frown.

"That isn't nearly enough."

I glance at the clock. There are still a few hours until The Divide falls, and there's that little Asian market a few blocks away. Plenty of time. I climb the stairs to the beat of the music, twirling into the bedroom. I pull on my sloth tank top, then hop around as I miss the right leg of my cut-off jean shorts twice. I hit the bed with a giggle, finally getting my shorts on. Jogging back downstairs, I slide my flip-flops on. With my bag slung across my body, I pop my earbuds in and grab my keys as I head out.

The sky is a beautiful canvas of purples and pinks and oranges with the fiery tip of the sun kissing the horizon. My music drowns out everything around me, filling me with happy beats. A woman walks by, head bowed, attention glued to her phone. A long leash trails behind her, a medium-size dog trotting along. His grey and white shaggy fur sways with each of his steps, his tail wagging like a flag. The dog looks up at me, his tongue lolling out in a cute doggy smile. He stops, and so do I. The woman doesn't look up from her phone as she pauses, assuming the dog is peeing or something. She's not paying attention. She stopped because the dog stopped. I have the urge to say something. It's such a beautiful evening, and she's out with the goodest boy, but she's glued to her phone ... like I used to be all the time.

I keep my mouth closed. Instead, I turn my music down as I crouch, only wobbling a little as I hold my hand out. The dog sniffs me, then gives me a little lick. I scratch his head, and he wags his tail faster. I smile as he leans into my scratches. I've always wanted a dog.

The woman finally looks over, and she tugs on the leash. "Oh, I'm sorry. Come on, Silks."

The dog trots to its owner, and I'm about to tell her it was okay, that I love dogs, but her attention is already back on her phone as she walks away, Silks in tow.

My bottom lip pouts out as I watch them leave, but I shake it off. Any day that I get to pet a dog is a good day. With a smile back on my face, I stand, holding my arms out to steady myself from the spinning in my head. I'm all floaty from the tequila. With a smile, I turn and smack into someone.

Damn it! Why do I keep running into people?

A deep masculine chuckle has me backpedaling, and I trip over my flip-flops. A large hand wraps around my bicep, steadying me before I fall on my ass. My gaze travels up a muscled torso wrapped in a form-fitting button up short-sleeve shirt. The top three buttons are undone to reveal mouth-watering bronzed skin. His throat bobs as he swallows, and my eyes continue their upward perusal over a smooth jaw, pink lips quirked in a smile that fills his cheeks. Startling silver eyes meet mine, his shock of black hair sweeping over his forehead.

Bookstore man!

My body heats, and I blame the hours in the sun and the alcohol swirling in my system, but I know a good portion of the pulsing warmth curling through me is due to the yummy snack standing before me.

In a daze, I slide my earbuds out and tuck them into my pocket. I blink up at him, and his smile stretches into a grin as he says, "If we keep running into each other like this, I'm going to think it's fate."

I blush, fighting the urge to fidget under his gaze. He's here, right in front of me. The man I've been imagining in my bed as I get myself off over and over and over ... He's here.

I know I'm staring, but I can't seem to stop. He's even more beautiful than I remember.

CHAPTER 9

MALICIOUS

I stop, heart racing. Every time I see her, I'm stunned. I can't believe she's real.

I stare at her crouched form. Her fingers scratch under a dog's chin, and I'm envious of the little creature. He looks so happy to be the object of Summer's affection. I need that ... her gaze on me, her hands on my body.

As the dog's owner pulls him away, I remain where I am, knowing I'm too close. Summer stands and spins, smacking right into my chest, and that brief contact makes my cock jerk.

With her standing right before me, bright green eyes blinking in the setting sun, Summer is even smaller than I recall. The little bikini string tied behind her neck and disappearing under her shirt tempts me. My fingers itch to give the end a little tug.

That's all it would take ...

When I drop my hand from her arm, Summer takes

another step back, and I almost grab her wrist to keep her close but stop myself at the last minute. She stuffs her hands in her pockets, the ends of which poke out the bottom of her cut-off shorts. Very short shorts. So much leg for someone so small.

The wind ruffles her dark hair as she blushes, adding color to her tan. Has she been laying in the sun all day? Suddenly, I'm jealous of the sun's rays that got to kiss her skin. Would she be salty if I licked her?

She shifts her weight to one hip, saying, "I don't know about us meeting like this being fate, more like alcohol. I'm sorry for slamming into you ... again."

I raise a brow with a teasing smile. "Day drinking?"

She laughs. "Yup! I'm on vacation after all. But let's not put all the blame on the tequila. That dog was soooo cute. I was rightfully distracted."

The alcohol has softened Summer. She's pliant, happy, sun-drenched, and oh so fuckable. I might as well be the angel the humans call my kind, because I'm somehow able to keep my eyes off her breasts under that thin tank top and on her face as I ask, "Do you have a dog?"

Her smile turns wistful. "Nah." Looking over her shoulder, she sighs at the far-off figure of the woman and her dog. "I love dogs. Just never had the time to properly take care of one. But maybe"—she turns back to me—"when I go back home, I'll look into adopting one."

I almost tell her she will not be going home, but I put my hands in the pockets of my light-weight pants, mirroring her. "So, where's home?" That must have been the wrong question because her expression closes off, her lips pressing together. And was there a flash of alarm in her eyes?

Fighting to keep my growl contained, I vow to

discover everything that causes my little sunshine even a drop of fear and vanquish them all.

Quickly, I wave off my words. "I apologize. That was terribly personal. We haven't even properly met." I hold out my hand, anticipation pulsing through me as I say, "My name is Mal."

Summer looks at my hand like it might bite her. I hold steady, giving her time, and finally a little smile slips to her lips, and she sways towards me. "Nice to meet you, Mal. I'm Summer."

Fuck. Hearing my name coming from her lips ...

Her small hand slides across mine, and my skin tingles from her touch, the sensation rushing up my arm and across my chest. Her skin is warm, and her grip is firm as we shake hands for a little longer than is necessary. I swear I feel her tugging at my heart.

Summer's gaze moves to my shoulder ... no, just beyond my shoulder, and her brows furrow before quickly smoothing out. She slides her hand from mine, and it takes enormous effort to let her go.

With a small smile, I say, "I admit to already knowing your name, Summer. I overheard Paine's ma—girlfriend use your name in the bookstore."

She nods, rubbing her hands together. "You and Paine are ...?"

What are we? "Paine and I are acquaintances." I pause, watching as she runs her fingers through her hair before I go on. "I'll admit, I was disappointed when Paine's girlfriend spirited you away so quickly."

Shifting her weight to her other foot, Summer blushes, biting her bottom lip. Fuck me. I've never wanted to kiss someone so badly. She glances beyond me, and I think she's getting ready to make her excuse to leave, so I blurt out, "May I buy you a drink?" Her shoulders tense up slightly, so I'm quick to add, "As an apology for running into you."

She chuckles, the tightness draining away. "You don't need an excuse to ask me out. I ... I'd love to. I've thought about you ... a lot since the bookstore." She slaps her hand to her forehead. "God, I can't believe I just admitted that."

I chuckle, drawing her gaze back to me where it belongs. "No need to be embarrassed. Seems we both made an impression on each other."

"You ... You've thought about me too?"

I nod, pressing my lips together before saying, "I have. I was on the verge of forcing Paine to arrange a meeting between us, but I was hoping I'd run into you again."

She laughs, throwing her head back, and the sound curls inside me, then spreads like the warmth of a sunbeam. "Well, I literally ran into you, again. Jesus, I swear I'm not usually this oblivious to my surroundings."

I laugh. "We can blame the alcohol and general dog cuteness."

Summer drops her gaze, shifting the little bag that's slung across her chest. Why does that stupid bag get to hug her breasts and I don't? Her voice draws my eyes back to her face as she says, "There's not much time before The Divide falls, so I don't think there's time for a proper date."

She blushes, but her comment reminds me. Damn. I don't have to worry about The Divide falling, but she certainly does. Well, not with me around, but she doesn't know that ... yet.

Summer continues, "Anyway, I was on my way to the Asian market. I need more limes. One can't make a decent margarita without fresh lime juice."

Stepping to the side, I hold out my arm. "Then, may I accompany you?"

"You want to come to the grocery store with me?"

Yes, more than anything. Well, not *anything*. What I really want is to steal her away to my castle, strip those little shorts off her legs, and untie her bikini with my teeth. Instead, I say, "If you wouldn't mind the company."

"Sure, I'd ... I'd like that."

Her flip-flops slap the sidewalk as she walks past me. I turn, matching her pace. We walk in silence for a while, and other than having to fight the urge to take her hand, it's pleasant. After about a block, I ask, "So, you said you're here on vacation?"

"A *long* overdue summer vacation."

"Well, I hope it's been good so far."

"Yes. So far, it's been just what I needed."

She glances at me, her eyes traveling down my body before a little blush blooms pink on her cheeks.

Yes, little Summer. I'm just what you need.

She returns her gaze forward, clearing her throat, and I hold back a chuckle. It's gratifying to know she's as affected by me as I am by her.

We approach the Asian market, and the doors automatically swoosh open, cold air blasting us. Summer shivers and goosebumps prickle her exposed skin. I want to wrap my arm around her, but I just follow along as she picks up a basket and slings it over one arm. She grabs a giant bag of limes, and as soon as she drops them in her basket, I take the handles, unthreading it from her elbow. She starts to protest, but I hold up a hand. "Please, allow me."

Her eyes sparkle with warmth as she nods. "Do you mind if I grab a few other things?"

"Not at all."

As we weave through the tight aisles, she sways every so often but stays upright. I wonder how drunk she is as I ask, "So, what are some of your favorite things to cook?"

Apparently, this was a good question, because she launches into descriptions, pointing at things as we pass, telling me how she likes to prepare them and what she serves them with. I don't really understand half of what she's talking about, but she's so animated and happy, I'd let her talk about food for hours just so I could hear her voice.

I'm thankful I thought to add the kitchen in my new house. The thought of us together, sauces simmering, the scent of rich food wafting around us, each of us taking the occasional sip from our drinks ... who knew cooking could be so sensual?

Damn. This woman has bewitched me. And I'm delighted by it.

She goes into great detail of how she makes her spicy margaritas, and all I can think about is licking the chili salt off her lips. When she grabs a bottle of red wine, I distract myself from the temptation of her sinful mouth by saying, "Did you know the ancient Greeks used to eat flatbread dipped in wine for breakfast?"

She wrinkles her nose, and I find the expression so cute, the need to kiss her has me leaning down before I catch myself. Damn it. All I want to do is kiss her until she's falling apart in my arms, begging me for more.

She puts the bottle in the basket, saying, "Good for the ancient Greeks, I guess. Doesn't sound all that appealing first thing in the morning."

I chuckle. What would she think if I told her stories of my life living among the ancient Greeks? A rich merchant gifted me the bronze laurel crown I still wear today with the hope that I'd marry his daughter. I enjoyed the daughter, and she enjoyed me and the *special* things I can do with my cock. The marriage didn't happen, but I kept the crown.

Coming out of my memories, I focus on Summer as she tells me about a pasta sauce she likes to make with the wine. We make our way to the front where she pays, and I grab the bag before she can. The heat of the day greets us, a welcome warmth after the chill of the store. She pauses a few steps away from the doors, holding out her hand, supposedly for her groceries.

"Thank you, Mal. This was fun. Grocery dates should be a thing."

I hug the bag to my chest, shaking my head. "My time is yours. I'm having a very nice time with you, Summer." And I am. I'm enjoying learning things about her. I like being near her. I'm ... content. How odd. "I'm not ready for it to end. May I escort you home?"

She doesn't drop her outstretched arm. A lick of fear shutters across her eyes. What has her spooked? What did I say?

Summer steps forward, and just then, a soft breeze brushes her from behind, bringing me her scent. Petrichor, smoke, and copper. My mouth waters, and now that I know what to look for, I taste her magic. It's buried deep, and I doubt she knows of her power, but it's delicious. I send out my own magic, searching for any threats that may be nearby. Not many monsters are strong enough to pass through The Divide before it falls, even with the summer solstice so close, but still, I worry.

She wraps her hand around the handle of the bag, tugging. "Thank you, but it's not far, and it's getting late. You should probably head home. You don't want to get caught outside."

Stubbornly, I hold the bag, keeping her close as I nod

89

in the direction of her townhouse. "Your place is on my way home."

Her eyes go wide. She abandons the bag, backing away quickly. I hold up a hand, moving to follow her, but I stop as she plants her feet and punches her fists to her hips.

Oh, angry Summer is glorious. I want to taste her fury. I want to kiss her through that temper.

She stands tall, which is still terribly short. She starts to pitch back, but catches her balance, keeping that stormy look in her eyes through the haze of her alcohol buzz.

I shrug unapologetically. "Paine's girlfriend told me where you're staying."

Technically, it's true since it was Mira shouting Summer's name into the night that alerted me to her being in that townhouse.

Summer's eyes go wide. Eyeing me, she opens her small bag with an angry *zip*. She digs out her phone, her finger tapping furiously. She pauses, then a soft chime comes from her device. As she scans the message, her shoulders relax slightly.

Looking up at me, Summer puts her phone away and sighs. "Seems Mira did tell you." I raise a brow, and she huffs, hands landing on her hips again. "Yes, I checked."

I nod. "Good."

Summer snorts. "Good?"

"Why take me at my word when it comes to your safety? It's okay to be cautious, Summer. It's smart."

A look that I can only describe as dreamy softens her eyes. "Ohhhh. Um. Okay."

My lips quirk with my suppressed chuckle, and I hold out my free arm. "So, shall we?"

She nods, turning. I follow my woman, unable to keep the grin from my face.

Looking over her shoulder, she slows so we walk side-by-side and asks, "So, Mal, tell me more about yourself. I've done all the talking so far."

"Hmm. Let's see. I love art."

"Anything in particular?"

I shake my head. "Not really. I don't care if it's a painting, a sketch, a sculpture ... I like ... the emotions captured in art. I love the rush of different feelings that well inside me as I get lost in something a huma—someone created with their hands." I don't think she noticed my almost-slip. Thank you, tequila.

What I don't say is that until her, art was one of the only things that stirred me out of my boredom, that brought a small amount of color to my grey existence.

Her eyes stay on me as we continue walking. "That's beautiful, Mal. I'll admit, I don't know much about art, but the way you talk about it makes me curio—"

With her attention on me, she misses the step-down of the curb. She stumbles into the cross street, and my arm snaps out. I grab her shoulder, pulling her back as a car slams on its brakes. The driver throws up their hands, an angry scowl on their face. I glare at them, and they quickly put their hands back on the steering wheel, slowly driving off.

Summer hasn't said a thing, but her back rises against the front of my body with her quick breaths. Leaning down, I inhale her scent, catching the sour taste of fear under the flavors of petrichor, smoke, and copper. Her skin prickles as I whisper against her ear, "Are you okay, Summer?"

She nods. "At this point you won't believe me, but I swear I'm not usually this clumsy." Turning slowly, she looks up right into my eyes. I expect her to back away, but she stays close. So fucking close.

My voice practically purrs from my throat. "Can I boost my ego and think it was my presence that distracted you this time?"

Her lips part, and she holds my gaze for a long second before looking down my neck, over my chest, and to the waistband of my pants. Licking her lips, she snaps her gaze back to my face. She's flushed, and all I want to do is take the tiny step to press our bodies together. She opens her mouth, but before she responds, her eyes lift to my hair, her head tilting. Reaching up, she stops short of touching me.

I can't read her expression, and it's driving me mad.

Summer squints, shakes her head, then her eyes go wide. Taking a step away from me, her heels dip off the edge of the curb, and her arms windmill.

Damn it, this woman is a hazard to herself.

I snatch her wrist, pulling her back on steady feet. Her gaze is glued behind me, her teeth worrying at her tempting bottom lip. What is she looki—

"You, y-you have ..." Summer lifts her free hand, pointing. "I'm not crazy. I'm not. My imagination is good, but this ..." She hiccups, running her hand through her hair. "You have wings!"

CHAPTER 10

MALICIOUS

Summer snorts, her finger still wagging at my wings ... which should be invisible to her. "I'm not that drunk. Or am I? I feel like Alice, and I've fallen down the rabbit hole into this town where I'm slowly going mad." Looking around, she gestures at a woman walking our way. "Hey, do you see this? The wings?"

The woman stops a few feet from us, her eyes dashing between Summer and me. Her brow furrows, and a fake smile that clearly says she's uncomfortable spreads across her face. "Um. I'm sorry. What? Wings?"

Summer's arm drops to her side as she looks over my shoulder, seeing what no one else can see. She gives the woman an apologetic wave. "Sorry. Nothing." Then she mumbles to herself, "I guess I am crazy."

I smirk at her frustration. My poor little witch. The woman starts to walk past us, trying to keep as much space between herself and us. Summer glares up at me. Her green eyes sparkle as she opens her mouth, ready I'm sure to demand I explain, but the woman pauses, looking closely at Summer as she says, "Are you ...? You're Summer, aren't you?" Her voice rises in excitement.

The look on Summer's face makes me want to wrap my wings around her, shield her, or better yet, carry her away from here. But the next moment, a fake smile lifts her lips, and she nods. "Yes. Hi."

The woman presses her hands to her cheeks and squeals. The only way I can describe her reaction is star-struck. I've seen that look of awe many times when I used to come to the human realm as the archangel Michael. Who exactly is my Summer?

The women shake hands. I stand behind Summer, unused to not being the center of attention. I realize I've zoned out as the woman asks, "What brings you all the way here? I saw your post about unplugging for a while, and I get it. Being on social media is draining enough, but for someone like you, I'm sure it's a lot." She waves her hands around excitedly. "I never in a million years thought I'd meet *The* Summer. I love all your content. You come across as so real."

I barely hold back my growl. *Summer* is *real, you twit.*

The woman goes on, "My bank account doesn't love you so much." She laughs, and Summer chuckles, but something about the sound seems forced. I don't think Summer is enjoying this interaction. I'm certainly not.

Before the woman can start speaking again, I step closer to Summer, towering over them both. My movement draws the woman's attention to me, and her eyes widen slightly as she stares at my face, then slowly works her gaze down my chest. I don't say a word, staring her down. She swallows, tearing her eyes from me and back to Summer. She reaches into her bag, and Summer takes a tiny step back towards me, her back pressing to my front. I nearly groan.

I feel tension snap up Summer's spine when the woman pulls out her phone and holds it up. "Can I take a picture with you?"

Without waiting for a response, the woman turns, backing up, pointing the screen back at us.

The woman's finger hovers over the little camera button, and Summer's words sound panicked as she turns her head to the side. "I'm s-sorry. I'd rather n-no—"

Rage has my glamoured wings snapping out, but Summer doesn't react—that's how rattled she is. I reach over both women, wrapping my large hand around the woman's phone, plucking it from her grip. She gasps and sputters as she turns. She looks like she's going to snap at me, but quickly closes her mouth as I glare at her.

I take a slow inhale, devouring the tangy scent of her fear and the lemony scent of her embarrassment as I say, "You realize you haven't stopped talking since you recognized Summer. You haven't let her speak or respond, and when she tried to tell you she did not want a picture, you were ready to ignore her and take it anyway. Is that how you treat someone you say you admire? You should be asha—"

Summer's hand squeezes my forearm, and my gaze falls to her. And I keep falling. I am hers. She's fully facing me, and her pink lips mouth, "Thank you." My skin prickles and warms as she runs her fingers down my arm, over my wrist, across the back of my hand, and down my fingers. She takes the phone, glues a smile on her face, and turns back to the woman.

Holding the phone out to the now silent woman, Summer says, "It was really nice meeting you ...?"

The woman takes the phone, gripping it until her knuckles turn white. She darts her gaze to me, a flicker of anger pinching her eyes before she quickly looks away as she says, "Paula."

Summer's voice sounds a little tight as she says, "I appreciate your compliments and your support, Paula. It really means a lot. I hope you understand. I am on vacation, unplugging for a bit as you know. Any other time, I'd be happy to take a picture with you, but I'm—"

I clear my throat. Summer shouldn't have to apologize or explain. I'm ready to be away from the annoying Paula. Summer glances up at me, her eyes darting over my shoulder to my wings. Looking back at Paula, Summer waves at the bag in my hand. "I'm sorry to rush off, but I need to get my groceries home."

Not waiting for Paula to respond, I place my hand on Summer's back, my fingers flexing against the thin material of her tank top. We move past Paula, but only make it a few steps before the artificial click of a camera sounds from behind us.

With a growl, I spin around. Summer reaches for me, but her fingers close around air. I'm in front of Paula in a heartbeat. My shadow engulfs her, and my growl deepens. The silver glow of my eyes reflects in her brown ones. My power grabs her, holding her immobile. Not knowing about real magic, humans call the sensation frozen with fear. This time I don't bother to take her phone from her hand. Instead, I wrap my fingers around hers and squeeze. She winces, then as I keep squeezing, tears fill her eyes. She tries to pull away but can't. Plastic cracks. Metal groans. Pieces of Paula's phone clink to the sidewalk. There's a loud pop as her phone screen shatters.

Paula yelps. "Ow! What the hel—"

Leaning over her, I get right in her face. "If you think you see Summer around town again, you don't."

I let her go, pleased at the red marks on her hand from

my grip. There's also blood on her palm from the broken glass. I don't give her a second look. Spinning around, I lick the smear of Paula's blood off my thumb. It gives me a little hit of power, but not much. If it were a few hours later, and The Divide was down, I'd kill Paula, consume her soul, and leave her body for the other monsters. But if The Divide *was* down, none of this would have happened because the humans would be hiding in their homes.

Wait, why am I holding back? Paula disrespected Summer. She deserves death.

Again, I'm halted by Summer's touch. Her small hand presses to my outer arm above my elbow. I look down at my little sunshine, most of my anger draining away. She shakes her head as if she can read my thoughts. "Thank you, Mal. Let's go."

With Summer's hand on my skin and her eyes on me, everything else fades away, even Paula who doesn't know how close she just came to death. Almost as if I'm in a daze, I follow Summer. I remain behind her, entranced by the sway of her hips as we walk the few blocks it takes to get to her townhouse.

Her flip flops slap against the first stair leading up to her door, and I panic. I need more time with her. I just need ... more.

Forever.

"Summer."

She turns, her foot still propped on the bottom step. I'd invite myself in, but I can't get past the blood-carvings. At least I can't until I make her mine. Soon enough.

Summer reaches for the bag of groceries, her eyes flicking over my shoulder. She hasn't mentioned my wings again. My grip tightens on the handles of the bag, and she stands there, arm held out, eyes on me. I can't help but wish she was reaching for me and not her groceries.

Slowly, she lowers her hand, her tongue sliding out to lick her lips.

Fuck. Me.

She whispers, "Mal."

I take a step closer, flaring my wings wide. Her gaze snaps to them, traveling the broad width. I let her look, my heart racing, my skin tingling. Eventually, her eyes come back to my face. Her cheeks are flushed, and her breaths are coming a little faster. I take another step, and she climbs fully onto the first stair. We're still not eye-to-eye, but it brings her closer. I search her gaze as she stands watching me with parted lips. She leans in.

Holy hell.

Blood surges to my cock. I think my heart actually stops. Her scent wraps around me with an added spice of ... tequila. That's right. My little sunshine has been drinking.

I'm not an angel after all.

My free hand slides around the back of her neck, her shaved hair tickling my skin as I pull her to me. Our lips meet. My world shifts. I have truly been living in darkness. Summer is light, sunshine, warmth, happiness ... mine.

She shifts, pressing her lips a little harder to mine, angling so her top lip slides between mine. With a groan, I suck her into my mouth, and when she gasps, I slide my tongue between her lips.

It's a slow kiss, our heads tilting side to side as we learn each other. Her hands grip my shirt, holding me to her. I'm so caught up in Summer, I don't realize I've let my glamour slip until her palms press to my bare chest. Quickly, I wrap myself back in my magic, clothing myself and vanishing my wings and crown just in case someone walks by, or a nosy neighbor looks out their window.

I pull back, aroused at the sight of her swollen lips. Her chest rises and falls, pressing her breasts against me. Fuck. A frustrated chuckle bubbles from my mouth. "Damn it, Summer. You are temptation in human form."

She grins, her gaze landing on my wings before returning to my face. "And you are ...?"

Before I can come up with an answer, a loud chime comes from her bag. Summer winces. "Sorry." Leaning back, she retrieves her phone. The screen lights up her face, and I have the urge to grab her phone and toss it away for taking her attention off me.

Whatever she sees on her screen darkens her gaze. Her fingers turn white as her grip tightens, and she starts trembling. I set the grocery bag on the ground and wrap my hands around her shoulders. "Summer, what's wrong?"

She shakes her head, bending down, bringing her mouth much too close to my cock. Grabbing her groceries, she stands back up. "I'm sorry. I need to take care of something, but I'd like to see you aga—" She's moving to put her phone away, but I grab it without thinking. Rising to her toes, Summer tries to take it back, but it's easy to keep it out of her reach.

I start reading, rage swelling quickly. "Wait. A stalker? Someone has been harassing you? This man?"

She jumps, reaching for her phone. So cute. She says, "Mal, don't. I'm dealing with it."

Turning the phone to face her, but not letting her take it back, my voice growls as I say, "This man, Henry Shillings, has been stalking you? And according to this email, it's not the first time he's done this."

She huffs. "If you'd give me back my phone, I could finish reading the email ... addressed to *me*."

"Summer, this is serious. He's harassed other women

101

before. Wait"—I read the signature at the end of the email —"Max. Vex's Max?"

"I don't know what a Vex is. Mal, give me back my phone."

All it takes is a thought. My magic surrounds us both, hiding us from view. My wings snap out, my laurel crown settling in place on my head. As I wrap my arms around Summer, I realize my clothes are gone once more. Probably not the best move right now, but I can barely think past the red haze of anger pulsing through my mind.

She squeaks as I launch into the air, aiming for my house. Surprisingly, she doesn't scream or struggle. She doesn't faint. She just holds on, looking behind me as she says, "I knew they were real." A laugh bursts from deep in my chest. Her gaze snaps to mine, a little pout on her lips. "What? You made me feel like I was crazy, like I was seeing things."

"You were seeing things you weren't supposed to be able to see. But that's just one of the very special things about you, Summer."

She bites her lip, and I duck, pressing a quick kiss to her mouth before slowing the beating of my wings to descend. As soon as my toes touch down, Summer still in my arms, she lets loose a stream of questions. "Special? Did you fix my windows? Why can I see your wings and other things? What are you? Are you from the monster realm? How can you be here when The Divide isn't down yet?"

I chuckle, reluctantly setting her on her feet. My hands land on her hips, and I stare down at my little sunshine. "Are you not afraid of me?"

She looks over my face, then shrugs. "Why would I be? You're still the kind, considerate man who went on a grocery date with me, listening to me ramble, and kissed me into oblivion ... you're that man, just with wings. Right?" Her head tilts. "And you're wearing a crown." She smiles, shaking her head. "Why does something so ostentatious look natural on you?" Her eyes dart down my body then snap back to my face, her hand held in front of her as if to block my cock from her sight. "And why are you naked?"

I laugh again, materializing clothes back on my body. "I usually only wear clothes when I'm 'human.'"

She hums with a wistful look in her eyes. "Yeah. No complaints. You are ..." She fans herself.

My laughter booms through the early evening, and she smiles at me with a blush staining her tan cheeks. I shake my head. "Ah, Summer. You are a delight."

She ducks her head, running her fingers through her short, wind-blown hair before looking back at me. "Ever since the bookstore, I've felt ... drawn to you. I kept looking for you every time I went out. And now, here you are, and you're ... I ... I like you, Mal."

And I would tear apart the fabric of time and space to be with you.

"I like you too, Summer." Though what I want to say is that my heart and soul belong to her now and forever. "This is my place. Please, come inside."

"Will I be safe? You know, if I'm ... if I'm still here when The Divide falls?"

That's the plan, little sunshine.

I turn to fully face her. My hands cup her cheeks, my thumbs caressing her skin. "Always."

CHAPTER 11

SUMMER

My earlier tequila buzz has almost completely burned off, and while I know I should be freaking out, I'm oddly calm.

Kissing Mal was ... Fuck. It was far better than all the times I imagined it would be. And then he flew us here. To his house. *Flew*. With his wings. His *real* wings.

I'm pretty sure he's an angel, but I'm afraid to ask. Angels are supposed to be scary, deadly, the worst of the monsters. But Mal is so ...

My face is still in his warm hands, and I feel my cheeks getting hotter as my blush deepens. He's so close as he whispers, "Summer?"

I nod as much as his touch will allow me. The next second, his lips are back on mine. It's a rush that makes my head spin and my pussy throb. He must be an angel to be able to kiss this well. This is expert level. My whole body is tingling. I'm about to come from a kiss.

Slowly, Mal pulls back, and I know I'm breathing hard, but I can't seem to slow my pounding heart. His eyes fall to my heaving chest, then he drops his hands from my face only to interlace our fingers. Leading me to the mid-century modern house before us, he opens one of the double front doors.

I take in the small, bright foyer, my brows furrowing. "How do you have a house in the human realm?"

Mal chuckles, taking me farther into his house. "I created it earlier this week."

I stop in the wide hall, and he turns to face me as I ask, "You created this house?"

He nods. "With magic. Monsters, like me, use magic for everything. It's our currency, energy, light ... it's the only thing worth anything in our realm."

His eyes search my face, for what? Fear? Does he think I'm going to run screaming into the night? I mean, I guess that would be a logical reaction, but again, there's an odd calmness within me that feels soul deep.

With his eyes glued to me, I walk past Mal, doing my best to keep my gaze from his pants that I now know conceals his ... impressive equipment. I saunter down the hall like I know where I'm going, and his soft footfalls sound behind me. I turn into the first room I come to. A living space. Modest but cozy. Large sliding glass doors look onto a manicured garden with the shimmering lake beyond. I take a second to appreciate the view as I take a seat on the soft sofa. Crossing my legs, I bounce my foot as I look up at Mal. In this position, he towers over me. It should be intimidating, but it turns me on.

My imagination wanders as I picture Mal leaning over me, bracing his hand on the back of the sofa as he presses his knee between my thighs. Swallowing, I say, "I have questions."

Pulling my bag over my head, I toss the crossbody on

the floor at my feet, just now realizing my groceries are still on the sidewalk outside my house. Oh well.

Mal smiles with a little shake of his head. Coming over, he sits next to me. I think about scooting closer to press my thigh against his, but I stay put. Instead, I shift sideways so I'm facing him. He does the same, his deep voice caressing every inch of my exposed skin as if it is a physical touch.

"Where would you like to start?"

Your hands on my naked breasts.

I hold out my hand. "Can I please have my phone back?"

With a frown, he places my phone in my waiting palm. I'm proud that my fingers only tremble a little as I reopen the email that I only got to read a part of before Mal took it. Max found my stalker, but that's not all. Max has attached a social media post to the message. When I open it, I stare at a woman's account I don't recognize. And there, her most recent post is a picture of me from a few days ago.

I'm in the park I've frequented several times this week. My gaze slides to the view out the patio doors. It's dark, but I know that park sits on the far side of the lake. Looking back down, I stare at the post. In the picture, I'm walking, my gaze turned towards the water. The woman tagged me with the caption: *I can't believe Summer is in my town. How cool! I wanted to say hi but chickened out. Maybe if I see her again, I'll find the courage to ask her for a photo of us together.*

I sigh with relief. The location isn't tagged. But when I look closer at the image, my breath catches in my throat. There in the background is the park sign. It's blurry, but ... yeah, if I zoom in, I can make out the name of the park, and worse, the name of the town.

I close my eyes for a moment. *It's okay. It was bound to happen eventually. I'm an ocean away from* him. My eyes dart to Mal who's sitting silently, waiting. Some of my panic ebbs. *Yes, it's okay. I'm with ... an angel. At least I think he's an angel. I'd say I'm pretty damn safe ... from my stalker at least.* But am I safe with the monster sitting on this sofa with me?

My inner voice shouts, *Yes!* Being around Mal feels like ... like the gentle lapping of waves glistening with moonlight.

I sigh, looking back at the email. I close the attachment and scroll down until I come to the image of a man from the chest up. He's wearing a plaid shirt, his brown shaggy hair falling around his ears. He's good looking, a small smile on his lips, a dusting of a beard covering his lower face.

So, this is him. My stalker. Henry Shillings. He looks so ... normal.

I read through Max's email.

Apparently, women have logged complaints against him before, but he's never been violent, so ... Max said he'd keep digging, and for me to try to put it out of my mind for now and keep enjoying my vacation.

With a sigh, I respond to Max's email, thanking him for his hard work and for being in my corner. With a whooshing sound, the email sends, and I turn off my phone, setting it on the cushion next to me.

Mal's voice startles me as he asks, "All done?"

I nod, and Mal runs his hand from my shoulder to my elbow, giving me a little squeeze. I can't read the expression on his face. He seems angry, but there's something else behind his eyes. Releasing me, he stands. "I promise, Summer, you are safe here, but do not leave my house. I'll only be gone for a few seconds, a minute at most."

"Wait. What?" I'm speaking to an empty room. Mal is gone. I bounce on the cushion, looking all around the room. Nothing. A thud sounds from where he was a second ago, and I yelp, my hand pressing over my racing heart as I spin around to see Mal has indeed returned. And he's not alone.

A furious blond man with bulging muscles rips out of Mal's hold. From the expression on the newcomer's face, I fully expect him to punch Mal. I'm startled again when a loud banging comes from the front door. I think I'm going to have a heart attack.

The stranger smirks at Mal, crossing his arms. "You better let Vex in before they start destroying stuff."

Mal rolls his eyes, waving his hand. A second later, a shimmery blue monster appears with a blur of movement. It stands between the blond man and Mal, and though it's not much taller than me, it looks at Mal like it's going to tear him apart as it snarls, "You dare take my mate from me?"

Mal tsks. "I needed to borrow him. I'm a nepha. I don't ask. I take."

Well, that answers that. Mal is indeed a Nephilim. An angel.

The purplely-blue monster growls. "How'd you get past my wards?"

Mal raises a brow, his expression clearly saying, *Like your paltry magic would stop me.*

The small monster turns to the blond man. "Are you okay, Max?"

My mouth drops open. *Wait, Max? My Max?*

Tired of being ignored, I stand, and everyone focuses on me. Mal comes to my side, standing so close I can feel the warmth of his skin.

Max steps around the shimmery monster, his eyes

wide. "Summer?" I blink at him, my brain refusing to catch up. "This is where you ended up for your vacation? Had I known, I would have arranged a meetup in person. Did you receive my latest email?"

I swallow around my dry throat. "*You're* Max?"

He nods, holding out his hand. I shake it as he says, "Nice to meet you."

Max drops my hand, backing up, wrapping his arm around the little monster's waist. "This is Vex, they are my mate."

Mate.

I smile at Vex. "Nice to meet you." Looking back at Max, I ask, "Are you human?"

He chuckles. "Yes." His beautiful blue eyes snap to Mal before landing back on me. "I take it this nepha hasn't told you anything?"

Mal growls, and I swear the sound reverberates through my pussy as he says, "*This nepha* will tell Summer everything she needs to know, but first, give me all the information you have on Henry Shillings."

Vex growls back. "I don't like your tone."

Mal scowls. "I don't like you."

I hold up a hand, silencing the room. "Okay. Enough. Everyone, sit down."

Surprisingly, everyone does; me and Mal back on the sofa, Max on a large chair with Vex perched on his lap. I already love the couple. A monster and a human. I glance at Mal before dropping my gaze. It's nice to know a pairing like that works. I recall the wings and horns I've thought I've seen on Paine. Is he ...? Is Mira dating a monster? Are they mates like Max and Vex?

I have so many questions, but it's hard to organize my thoughts with the heat roiling through my core, my pulse thundering in my pussy, and my brain all fuzzy with the desire to kiss Mal again.

The delicious angel next to me leans back, crossing an ankle over his knee. His hand lands on my thigh, his thumb tracing little circles on my skin. It's very distracting. I should shift out from under his touch, but I don't.

Mal's voice carries around the room with an implied command. "I'd like to get this settled, so I'll quickly cover the basics." He looks at me, his expression softening. "I'll explain everything in more depth later, I promise." Mal holds my gaze until I nod, then turns back to Max and Vex. "As I understand it, Summer has a stalker. She hired Max to help tighten her security as well as to uncover the identity of said stalker, and you have found him. Correct?"

Max and I nod.

Mal continues. "There is something, a gem, in this town that is drawing monsters and their mates together, and I believe that is why Summer inexplicably ended up here out of all the places she could have chosen."

Wait. Me?

Vex opens their mouth, but Mal waves them off, continuing, "And that gem is what brought Max and Vex together as well as Paine and Mira."

I straighten. Seems I was right. Still, I ask, "Paine is ...?"

Vex answers me. "Paine is a dremar. If you were to see his real form, you'd probably call him a gargoyle."

I nod. "Hm. That explains the wings and horns."

Max leans forward, wrapping an arm around Vex, his fingers tracing over the waistband of their leather kilt as he says, "Wait, you can see Paine?"

All I can do is nod, my thoughts racing too fast from one question to another. Absently, my finger strokes along the barely-there line where I'd cut myself. The room is silent for a few seconds before Vex says, "Max and I weren't here the other night, but I heard about the attack on your home. That must have been scary."

My eyes flick to Mal before I drop my gaze to my healed hand. Vex's voice is gentle as they ask, "What happened, Summer?"

I press my fingers into my palm. "I, um, I was keyed up. Wide awake. It was strange, like pure energy laced through my blood. I needed something to do. I ... I was sharpening the kitchen knives when I cut my hand. It was really bad. I should have needed stitches." Holding up my hand, I show the others. "But it was like this the next morning."

Mal takes my hand, stroking my skin with his fingers. He might as well be stroking my clit as pleasure erupts through my core. I manage to keep my groan from escaping and barely hear his words. "You are special, Summer. Your blood contains old magic. I believe you are a descendant of a powerful line of witches, and that jewel I mentioned before may be drawing your magic to the surface. Not many witches remain in the human realm these days, and monsters will be drawn to the power inside you, especially when you bleed."

My mouth drops open, but Mal is quick to add, "Your blood-carvings will hold, and I will always ..."

He trails off, and my mind fills in the rest. *I will always be here for you. I will always protect you.* Is that what he was about to say, or is that just what I want him to say?

When I look up from our joined hands, the tightness in my chest loosens slightly, and I'm able to take a slow breath as I ask, "How are you, Max, and Paine able to be in our realm when The Divide is up?"

Max answers this time. "Apparently, it's a big secret, but the bond of true, fated mates breaks the magic of The Divide that separates humans and monsters."

I cock my head. "A true mate bond?" I look at Mal, anger curling my fingers into the cushion. "So, you can cross into the human realm because you ...? But you kissed me! You ... you made me feel ... who is your mate? How could you do this to them?"

Vex turns into Max's chest, and I swear I hear a little chuckle.

Mal's lips pull into a sexy smile as his eyes bore into mine. He practically purrs, "I am powerful enough to come through The Divide without the mate bond. During a time of power, like the approaching summer solstice, it's easier for someone as powerful as me." He pauses, uncrossing his legs, leaning closer. "But to answer your original question. I would never betray my mate." His voice dips even lower. "Because it's you."

The room is so silent, I can hear my heart beating.

Me?

Before I can process what Mal just said, he swivels, facing Max and Vex. "Max, were you able to find the stalker's address?"

The blond man nods, leaning over without dislodging Vex from his lap. Pulling a phone from his back pocket, he unlocks the screen, taps it a few times then holds it up facing outwards.

My brain is still scrambling. Maybe I'm still drunk? I feel like I've been three steps behind since I arrived at Mal's house.

Mal squeezes my thigh, stands, reads whatever is on Max's phone, then ... disappears. I stare at the empty space and Vex chuckles. "You look a little shell-shocked."

Max wraps his other arm around Vex, resting his chin

on their shoulder as he asks me, "Would a drink help or hurt?"

I shake my head. "Um, I did a little day drinking today. I'm half-convinced that I passed out on the roof hours ago, and this is all in my head."

Max laughs. "I like you. You'll be okay."

I relax a little. Kicking off my flip flops, I tuck my legs under me to sit crisscross. After a short silence, I ask, "Mal said it was me, right? I didn't imagine that?"

They both grin at me, and Max says, "You heard him right."

I look between them. "What does that mean, exactly?"

They exchange a look, but before either answer, Mal reappears. I jump with a little scream. "Jesus, Mal. You gotta quit jack-in-the-boxing in and out of here. I'm going to have heart failure."

Max laughs again, but my attention follows Mal's movements. He lifts his arm, opens his hand, and something falls with a wet splat to the distressed wood of the coffee table in front of me. I stare at the object, not sure what I'm looking at. I uncross my legs, planting my feet to lean forward.

Max swears, "Oh, shit."

I freeze. Is that ...?

An eye. An eye with the nerve still attached. Clear, viscous liquid and blood smears the table. Mal takes his seat next to me, crossing his ankle back over his knee, looking all too pleased with himself. The first warning siren goes off as he says, "Henry Shillings will find it hard to stalk you or anyone else without his eyes."

This might be one thing too much. I think I'm going to pass out.

CHAPTER 12

MALICIOUS

One problem sorted.

Summer's gaze darts between the coffee table and me, her face looking a little pale. I shift, leaning forward slightly. Her eyes find mine and hold as I say, "He looked at you. He watched you. He made you feel unsafe. He didn't deserve his eyes."

She blinks. "Wait. Eyes? Where's the other one?"

Under his breath, Max says, "Bet on getting to top next time that he ate it."

Vex chuckles.

I grin as I say, "I ate it."

Max kisses Vex on the neck, whispering something.

Summer stares open-mouthed at me. "You ate it?"

I nod. "Yes. He didn't deserve them, and I wasn't about to waste the magic."

She rolls her eyes dramatically, waving at the table. "So what, you saved that one for dramatic effect?"

"Exactly." I lean forward, pluck the eye up, and pop in my mouth. She shudders, gagging. I don't know what the big deal is. It's not like I'm chewing on it like a grape. My magic simply dissolves the eye into power that I then absorb.

I realize the room has been quiet for a few minutes, and when I look at Summer, she's staring at the little wet spot on the table. Leaning forward, I use my thumb to wipe it away. That seems to break Summer's daze as she says, "Is he dead?"

"Do you want him to be dead?"

She pauses, which I appreciate. She's actually thinking it through instead of saying what she thinks she should say. Shaking her head, she runs her hands through her hair. "No. I mean the petty, angry part of me says yes, but ... no?"

Taking her hand in mine, I rub my thumb over her knuckles as the second alarm blares from outside. "Well, he was alive when I left him."

She tilts her head at me, her eyes narrowing. "Explain."

I grin, and for a moment I consider kissing her instead of answering, but I say, "After I removed his eyes"—I curl a wing into my lap, stroking the metallic feathers—" I sliced into him. A shallow cut for every picture he had of you. As I said, there were a lot." I meet her gaze, knowing there's darkness in my eyes. I want her to see it. "My feathers were dripping with his blood."

She swallows, holding my gaze. After a tension-held moment, I sit back with a satisfied grin, saying, "Then, I knocked him out and left him in his backyard. The scent of his blood will draw the monsters. Even if he wakes up before The Divide falls, he's blind and has no idea where he is. As far as he knows, I left him in the middle of a field. Maybe he'll get lucky and find his way to the safety of his house, but I'm hoping he doesn't."

Summer takes a slow, deep breath. Her skin is still too pale for my liking, so I add, "Do you want me to go back? I can toss him into his house. Behind his blood-carvings he'll be safe from the monsters at least. I don't think he'll bleed out. Probably."

She stares at me for several long moments before a tiny smile twitches her lips. "I mean, The Divide will fall any second now, and going all the way back seems like a lot of work ..."

Throwing back my head, I laugh, and her melodic giggles join in. Max and Vex chuckle with us. As our laughter fades, the tension from earlier fades with it. Summer shakes her head, letting that motion travel down her body like a dog shaking water from its fur.

Settling into the couch cushion, she looks around at us with a little droop of her shoulders. "Okay. There's too much in my head. This is ... a lot."

Max laughs. "Yeah. I get that. But I must say, you are taking all this quite well."

Summer bites her lip, and I scoot closer until our knees touch. She doesn't move away, and I nearly vibrate with joy. She says, "Ignoring the eyes for now ... Okay, so monsters can live among humans without wanting to ... eat us?"

My cock twitches, and Vex grins as they say, "Define 'eat'."

Summer blushes, and I squeeze her hand. "Yes. About half of monster species *are* higher beings. We *can* exhibit self-control, unlike the more animalistic species. Most of the time we don't, but we can."

Summer's lips quirk in a smile as she nods, saying, "And you can come to the human realm even when The Divide is still up."

As if on cue, the final siren blares, and The Divide

falls. I nod. "Like I said, it's easier during a time of power."

"Like the summer solstice."

"Exactly. It's all about power. It takes an incredible amount of magic to fight against the pull of The Divide. Most monsters can't even push through a finger or claw."

She looks at Vex who shakes their head. "I could not."

Summer's gaze darts to Max then back to Vex. "And it's your bond with Max that allows you to travel freely between realms."

Vex and Max nod, then Vex adds. "Same for Paine."

Ducking her head, Summer looks at our joined hands. "You said I was your ... is that the reason for this ... insta-lust?"

Vex, Max, and I all answer at once. "Yes."

Summer nods. "Cool. Cool. Cool. Yeah. Cool. Okay. Yeah. I'm a witch. Monsters are bonding with humans. I'm ... Mal is ... Fuck."

I think she's starting to panic ... or the panic is finally pushing through. Shifting a little closer, I lean over her, flaring my wings, shielding her from Vex and Max as I whisper, "Slow breaths, little sunshine. You're doing great."

She keeps her head bowed but looks up at me through her lashes. "You really took my stalker's eyes."

It wasn't a question, but I nod anyway. "He screamed and begged as I burned the photos off the walls of his shed. He whimpered and promised me all sorts of things."

"Pictures? How'd you get in? Were there no blood-carvings on the shed?"

There were not, and I couldn't believe my luck when I found Henry in his unprotected shed and not in his shielded house. As I recall the hundreds of photos of Summer plastered all over Henry's walls, rage builds inside me once again. There were other women's pictures too, but Summer was the focus.

I realize I'm gripping her hand too tight and force myself to calm down.

Before I'm able to answer her questions, she holds up her free hand. "Never mind. I don't need to know. I don't *want* to know. He doesn't get to take up any more space in my mind or my life."

Good girl.

Vex says, "We're going, unless you need anything else, Malicious."

Summer chokes, coughing. "Mal is short for Malicious? Really? Malicious."

A smile quirks at my lips as I lean out of her space, closing my wings, and waving my hand at Vex and Max. "Go on then."

Max rolls his eyes, his voice dripping with sarcasm. *"You're welcome."*

I raise a brow at him, but he just chuckles. Vex follows their mate towards the hall but pauses and turns to face me. "If you touch my mate again, I'll spend the rest of my days figuring out how to kill you."

Max wraps an arm around Vex's chest, his eyes going dark as he whispers in the midnight monster's ear. "So violent."

Vex sneers, but blushes. "I mean it."

The two turn into the hall, and a second later the click of the door signals they've left. Summer's fingers pick at the frayed edges of her shorts. I want to know what she's thinking. A lot has been thrown at her, but she's oddly calm. I wait to see if she'll break the silence. I want to give her room to think, to process.

The minutes tick by, and finally, I crack. "Are you hungry?"

She blinks up at me, her eyes darting between mine. Her tongue flicks out, licking her lips before she bites the inside of her cheek. She nods, and I chuckle, shifting to adjust my now painfully hard cock. "Look at me like that, Summer, and the food will have to wait."

Her pupils widen, and the flush in her cheeks spreads down her neck to the top of her chest. Fuck. My wings flutter, and I lean in. Our lips are so close, I can once more smell the tequila on her breath. Her stomach rumbles, and I sit back with a smile. "Food."

She glances towards the kitchen, and I shake my head. No need. I wave at the coffee table, and a small spread appears. Crackers, cheese, fruit, meats. There's also a tall bottle of sparkling water with two glasses. Summer looks over the food, then turns to me with a little smirk. "Why even have a kitchen?"

I shrug. "I thought you might like one." Her mouth drops open, and I rush to add, "Not that a woman's place is in the kitchen. I just thought having a traditional human home would be comforting for you. I ... shit ... I can get rid of—"

Summer laughs, and my anxiety drains away. "Can I do magic like that?" I cock my head to the side and lean forward to drag my nose up her neck. She gasps. "What are you doing?"

Sitting back, I shrug with a grin. "Scenting you. Your magic is powerful, but old and diluted probably over many, many generations. I doubt you'll be able to use your power to this extent, but you did heal yourself without the actual knowledge of how to do so. So, who knows? I have a feeling you will continue to surprise me, sweet Summer."

To keep myself from kissing her, I reach with my free hand, collecting a cracker and a slice of buttery cheese.

Holding it out to her, I wait for her delicate fingers to brush mine to take the food. Instead, she leans close and holds her lips open.

I know there's heat blazing from my eyes—I can see their silver reflection in hers as I slide the cracker and cheese into her mouth. She bites, crumbs falling down the front of her shirt. Summer keeps her eyes on me as she chews.

This woman is going to be the death of me.

I love it.

She swallows, and I watch her throat flex. She'd look lovely swallowing my cock. I'm so distracted by the long line of her neck, I nearly jump out of my seat when her lips close around my fingers, taking the rest of the cracker and cheese. She sucks on me as she pulls back.

"Fuck, Summer. You are—"

She holds up a hand, chewing, then swallowing. My laurel crown thuds to the floor as Summer launches herself at me. Her arms wrap around my neck, her fingers brushing the feathers where my wings meet my back. A shiver trembles through my body as she climbs into my lap, straddling me.

I'm overwhelmed. My hands are everywhere, but I can't seem to touch enough of her. I need more. Our hips grind together, and a growl rips from my throat. She arches back with a moan, and my lips can't help but fall to her throat. As I kiss my way to her jaw, I earn my angel status as I say, "Summer, I'm on the edge of losing control."

Sitting up to look at me, her hips continue to roll against my hard length as she pants, "I do have one question."

My fingers dip under the hem of her tank top, tracing

over the skin of her lower stomach. Her eyes flutter, and I grunt. "Ask."

"Will my birth control work with you? I don't want angel babies flying around that can glow and might want to eat people."

I laugh, rubbing my palms up her sides. She gasps as I brush the outer edge of her bikini-clad breasts. "I don't know if human birth control works with monsters, but my kind can only reproduce with other nepha through a mutual sharing of our magic. It's transactional. Literally. Nepha create a spark of new life by intertwining their magic with a handshake."

"So why do nepha have sex?"

I laugh. "Because it's fun and it feels good."

She giggles. "Guess I walked into that one." Her smile drops, and she stops moving. My fingers press into her flesh as she says, "So you can only have babies with one of your kind? Then, why would I be ... mated to you? Are you sure that I'm ... that it's me ...?"

I wrap my arm around her back, my fingers tangling in the strings of her bikini. My lips press to her cheek, and I inhale her scent mixed with sweat and salt from her hours in the sun. "Being mated isn't about reproduction. It's about you and me. No one else. Nothing else. Just us." I kiss her other cheek. "So, yes, Summer. I'm sure." I kiss her forehead, and she relaxes a fraction. "And I'm delighted with the woman fate has chosen for me." I kiss her temple, and her hips press tighter to mine. "I've got you. I don't need kids. In fact,"—I kiss her nose—"I don't want them, unless you do, then we will find a way." I meet her gaze. "I like the idea of having you all to myself. I don't want to share you with anything or anyone." My lips press to hers. "You are all mine."

Her fingers curl into my hair at the base of my neck,

her green eyes staring into my silver ones. I can't read her expression, and my lips dip in a frown. "Too much?"

She sputters, snorting a little laugh that startles me. She laughs louder at my response, throwing her head back. "It's hard to wrap my head around all this craziness, but ... I ... I want it. I want it all to be true ... my magic, us being fated. You are just too perfect, like you were made for me."

"I was."

All it takes is a little press of my hands to her back, and she's flush against me. Our lips collide, our tongues tangling. Her little mewls accompany the squeezing of her thighs around my hips. I grip her adorable sloth shirt, nearly tearing it as I pull it over her head. Her breasts fill her little bikini, the mounds rising temptingly with each of her rushed inhales. Pitching her backwards, I lay her on the sofa, kissing my way down her body. I can't believe this is happening. I can't believe I've found her.

I say a silent thank you to the jewel sitting deep under my house.

With one foot on the floor and the other tucked under me, I sit back, staring down at my mate. She's flushed and panting, her thighs parted around me. So fucking beautiful. I grip her waist, and with a flex of muscle, I flip her over. She squeaks with a chuckle as I lean over her. I press my lip to her neck, and she grinds into the cushion as she moans, "Mal."

Just as I'd imagined, I grip the string of her bikini in my teeth and tug. With a soft whisper, the tie comes undone, and I immediately move my way down her back until I come to the next tie. This one falls away too.

"Summer, tell me your fantasies." I wrap my hand under her body, my fingers brushing over her navel before finding the button of her shorts. "Tell me what you desire." She lifts her hips to give me room to unzip her, the movement raising her ass towards me like an offering. My hand dives into her bikini bottom, finding her dripping and swollen. "Fuck, sunshine, you are already so wet."

I circle her clit before slipping one finger inside her. She moans into the sofa, grinding on my hand. Her words are muffled as she says, "I've been a needy mess ever since I ran into you at the bookstore."

My cock throbs, and with a thought, all my clothes disappear. I pull my finger from her pussy. The scent of her arousal causes pre-cum to drip from the head of my dick onto her back. I press my palm to the sticky mess and rub it into her skin. I want her to smell of me for days, even after she washes.

As I work her shorts and swimsuit bottoms down her legs, her ass squirms, and I want to bite it.

Summer is finally naked, and when I grip her waist, my hands span across her entire back. Lifting her hips, I position her so I can line my cock up at her glistening entrance. I nudge against her without penetrating, and she tries to shove back onto me. I chuckle, but the sound comes out hoarse with my need for her. Rubbing against her again, I say, "How do you want me, mate?"

Her body tightens, her pussy pulsing as she clutches at the cushion under her. Leaning all the way over her until my lips brush her ear, I say, "Does my little sunshine like it when I call her mate?"

She nods into the sofa with a moan that's on the edge of a sob. "Fuck, Mal. I've never ... I'm on fire. I ..."

My cock rubs between her slick folds. "Too much?"

She wiggles her ass against my stomach. "Not enough. I need ..."

"Tell me."

"I need you to fuck me. Hard, Mal. I need you to break me. I want—"

We both grunt as I ram into her, my balls slapping against her as I bottom out. I don't give her time to adjust before I start pounding into her.

CHAPTER 13

SUMMER

The soft fabric of the sofa rubs against my face as I'm shoved into the cushions over and over. Mal's thrusts hit me deep in a steady rhythm, driving my pleasure higher. The wet sounds of him sliding in and out of me are loud, and I groan.

Mal's voice whispers above me. "Fuck, Summer, you look glorious like this. Watching you take me is the loveliest sight I've ever seen. No singular piece of art on this planet can compare."

Turning my head to the left, my cheek presses into the sofa with each of his thrusts as I try to look at him. I want to see. I need to experience him in this moment.

Mal runs his large hand from my shoulder to my wrist, pressing his chest to my back. He curls over me with his much larger body, licking the shell of my ear. My body convulses, my pussy clenching around his cock. My thighs flex, my back arches.

Mal chuckles as he grips my arm. "So responsive."

"I ..." His thrust punches deep. "Want ..." He rolls his

hips, hitting new pleasure zones. "To see …"

His teeth graze my neck, and I buck under him as he says, "Yes, my sunshine."

I'm left empty and clenching around nothing as he pulls back. Using his grip on my arm and waist, he flips me. It happens so fast, the room spins, and I land on my back with an *oomph*.

For a long second we stare at each other, chests heaving with our rapid breaths. Jeeeesus. He's huge. How did that not tear me apart? Pre-cum drips from the glistening tip, dripping down his beautiful length, mixing with my arousal that's coating him. Licking my lips, I understand his earlier sentiment. He's gorgeous. Michelangelo's statues don't hold a candle to Malicious' perfectly chiseled body.

The v of his hips cuts a clear direction to his impressive cock, his abs rippling with each breath. He chuckles, gripping himself. "Wait until you see what else my cock can do."

My eyes widen as his corded legs brace my thighs open. His arm muscles flex as he reaches for me. My breath catches as his palms caress the skin along my inner thighs, slowly making his way to my throbbing pussy.

I lick my lips again, and Mal groans. "The way you look at me, Summer. I would tear The Divide down to have your gaze on me like this."

Heat scours through me. "Mal. Malicious. Please."

He goes still, his eyes going impossibly darker. A deep sound reverberates around me, sending chills across every inch of my skin. His chest actually vibrates as a growl rumbles up this throat, his lips peeling back in a terrifyingly predatory look.

Should I be afraid? Because I'm not.

I've never been more aroused in my life.

I try to squeeze my thighs together, needing something to relieve this growing tension inside me, but his hands and legs keep me spread for him. His growl continues as he leans over me. Mal's voice is pure sin as he says, "Say it again."

My brain is melting under all this pleasure. I need ...

What did he say? What does he want? I'll give him anything if he'll just fuck me.

One of my hands cups my breast, flicking and pinching my nipple. My other hand grips one of his wrists, trying to pull him to me. I need the vibration of his growl pressed against my skin. I don't care how needy I sound when I whimper, "Mal, ple—"

His arm snaps out, his hand wrapping around my throat. With a tug, I'm jerked upright until I'm directly under his piercing silver gaze. His wings flare, and his eyes start to glow. He's frighteningly beautiful. An angel. My angel. This close, his growl is stronger, but the breath of space between us keeps the delicious vibrations from touching me like I crave. Mal's voice brushes against my face.

"No, Summer. Say it. Say my name and tell me what you desire."

Oh. Ooooh. I swallow around my suddenly dry throat, holding his gaze as I say, "Malicious"—his eyes roll back before they lower back to my gaze—"I need your cock inside me. I need your growl pressed to my chest. I need you to surround me with your body, your wings. I need you, Malicious."

His growl stops. The room goes silent. I'm penetrated by his hungry stare, and I nearly come from the look of possessive adoration on his face. I swallow the moan in my throat and force my body to remain still even though all I want to do is rub myself all over his bronze body.

Finally, a softer vibration resumes in his chest as he whispers, "Already. You are already my everything."

Emotion stings my eyes, but I refuse to look away. He keeps his hand around my throat, his thumb doing delicious strokes against my skin. His other arm scoops under me, lifting me with ease. I wrap my legs around his waist as he stands, and I shiver at the sensation of his metal feathers caressing my skin.

Mal notices my reaction, and as he carries me across the living room, he curls his wings to touch more of me. I'm about to ask if his bronze wings are heavy, but the question tumbles from my mind as the entire house shakes. A frightened squeak leaves my throat as I curl into Malicious. Art falls from the walls, plaster and drywall cracks. Mal lifts a wing to shield me from a large chunk of ceiling as it breaks loose.

Panic steals all my logic. Something is coming. I kick and struggle against Mal's hold. I grip his hand and tug. "We need to go. We need to get out of here. Come on, Mal!" I'm shouting. My body is screaming at me to run, to go far, far away.

Mal throws us against a wall, curling his body around me as the entire roof rips away. Malicious' skin hardens, turning to actual metal. It sounds like rocks hitting a copper pot as pieces of the house crash against him. I can't breathe, and it's not just because Mal is holding me so tightly. I don't know what I'm looking at, all I know is I've never known true terror until right now. Shadows and smoke, dark skin, rippling muscles, glowing white eyes ... whatever this is, it completely fills the open space over Mal's house. It shifts and the earth shakes. A deep rumble makes my bones ache as the enormous being speaks.

"Thief."

The voice resounds, filling me with dread. Wetness

trickles down my face from my ears, and when I wipe at it, my fingers come away bloody. Taking me with him, Malicious hits the floor so quickly, his knees crack. Holding me against his chest, he bows, curling around me as he whispers, "I didn't know."

The being repeats, "Thief."

Tears prick my eyes. We're going to die.

Terror floods my body as I peek through Mal's feathers. A clawed hand the size of a bus is reaching for us. I want to scream, but nothing comes out. The floor bucks and trembles as the gigantic monster moves again. It's like a violent earthquake, and Mal's body is thrown into the air. He spins, landing on his back with a grunt, protecting me once again.

Pressure crushes me from every direction. Power. Magic. I'm suffocating. As the being points one of its claws at us, the thunderous voice says, "You have taken something from me, Malicious, so I will take something from you."

Mal scrambles, dropping me. I don't have time to care that I'm still naked as he shoves me behind him. The enormous being smashes the entire back of the house, and I'm able to see more of it. It's all I *can* see. It's impossibly big, like a mountain ... a terrifying, living mountain. There's only dark, rippling skin, shifting smoke, and flexing limbs. And those glowing eyes staring at me.

Malicious bellows, wings spread wide to shield me. "No! Wait! Ancient One, plea—"

Pain explodes from my head to the soles of my feet. I think I'm on fire, or being electrocuted, or being ripped apart. Or all three at once.

My legs buckle, and I reach for Mal's wing, but my vision tunnels. I collapse as the agony steals my breath.

CHAPTER 14

MALICIOUS

A cry tears from my throat, "No! Summer! Please, no!"

I've fucked up. I promised Summer she'd be safe. Fuuuuck. Tears stream down my face, tinkling against the hard metal of my skin as I do the stupidest thing I've ever done in my very long life ... I turn my back on the ancient.

Kneeling, I cup the back of Summer's neck, pulling her to my chest. Sobs rip painfully from my throat as I rock back and forth. "No, no, no, noooo."

I can't help but flinch from the pain scraping against my skin as the ancient speaks, much closer than before. "You are lucky, Malicious. Your mate isn't dead. She should be. She would be if she were merely human. But it seems the magic in her blood saved her ... this time."

Sliding my fingers around Summer's throat, the edges of my vision start to tunnel when I feel the faint fluttering of her pulse. I take a few deep breaths, relief giving me strength. Keeping my eyes averted, I tuck Summer tighter into my embrace as I turn on my knees. Bowing low over her slack body, I press my head to the splintered wood planks. "I didn't know, Ancient One. I swear it. I don't even know what it is. Take it."

The silence stretches, but I don't dare lift my head. I've angered an ancient. There are only four living ancients, and none of them have left their lairs in ages. And now, not only has this one emerged, but he has come to the human realm because *I was curious*. I was bored and just had to poke my nose where it didn't belong.

Fuck.

The ground rumbles with slow, approaching thuds. I don't move. I barely breathe. An agonizing sting prickles my skin as the ancient speaks from right before me. "I will not go fetch what is mine, what you stole. You will retrieve it for me. You will leave your mate, here ... with me, and you will bring me the stone."

My body doesn't want to cooperate, but against everything screaming inside me, I manage to lay Summer on the ground, materializing a blanket to drape over her naked, unconscious body. My knees tremble as I stand.

The ancient has changed his form. I'm not sure what his true form looks like. I don't think anyone knows. This ancient is so old, I wonder if he even remembers his original form.

His dark, smoky body is now small enough to fit in my destroyed living room, though the many sharp points of his horns—as thick as young tree trunks at the base—still spear above where my roof used to be. Dozens of white eyes that go from his bony forehead and down his foremost horns stare unblinking at me. Two of his arms sit across his chest, the other two are bent at his sides, hands on his hips. His scaled tail curls and whips around him, smoke trailing the movement, concealing his form from the knees down. His black lips pull back, exposing his obsidian fangs.

The ancient's chest glows red, and more smoke billows from his mouth as he commands, "I'm waiting, Malicious."

I take a step, and it feels like my heart cracks. I can't leave Summer with him, but I have to. Another step nearly takes me to my knees. Somehow, I shuffle over the wreckage of my home. By the time I reach the concealed door in my bedroom, I'm scrambling. I don't bother taking the stairs, jumping, spreading my wings as much as I can to fly all the way down. My feet don't touch the floor as I swoop through the safe room, snatching the gem. The stone burns, even with my hardened, metal skin. I don't care. I shoot back up to the main floor, gritting against the shout building in my throat as the skin of my hand melts, bronze molten metal splashing to the ground in my wake.

The pain fades, and a growl erupts from me when I see the ancient leaning over Summer. The way his enormous shoulders shift, it looks like he's ... touching her. With a flex of my wings, I fly over him, spinning, then spreading my sharp wings wide as I drop between the ancient and my mate. "Do not touch her!" My feathers slice through his skin. I grunt in pain as his molten blood scorches me, Smoke swirls around where I struck him, repairing in an instant any damage I did.

The ancient chuckles, the deep sound making my head feel like it's splitting apart. He holds out a hand. His long, boney fingers tipped with lethal claws, drip smoky magma that sizzles on the floor. I stand tall, shielding Summer, but keep my gaze averted as I drop the gem in the ancient's waiting palm.

Slowly, he curls his fingers around the stone.

Please leave. Please leave.

But he doesn't. The ancient looms over me, and I nearly choke on the brimstone and smoke curling around me, but I don't dare make a noise as he says, "Enjoy your mate, Malicious. I'm glad she survived your mistake."

I swallow, willing my body to stay upright. I'm trying not to show the trembling I feel deep inside, but I don't know if I'm succeeding. The smoke fades, and fresh air enters my lungs. Still, I don't move. The ground rumbles with a thud, then another, and another, each getting farther away. Even after silence falls, I count to ten, then twenty.

On a sob, I spin around and collapse before Summer. I rip the blanket off her, running my hands over every inch of her skin. She's okay. She's unharmed. A healthy pink has even come back to her cheeks, chasing away the deathly pallor from before. I pull her into my lap, rocking as I stroke her hair.

"I'm sorry. I'm sorry. I'm so, so sorry, Summer. Please wake up. Please, show me those beautiful eyes. I'm sorry. I'm sorry."

CHAPTER 15

SUMMER

I thought his feathers would be hard, but they are surprisingly delicate. The thought floats through my mind as I'm dragged from the darkness into consciousness.

Wait, what happened?

I'm sore all over like I ran a marathon, then did a thousand squats, then let someone use me as a punching bag. As I focus on my aching body, a warmth spreads through me like a bath slowly filling with steaming water. After a few moments, I feel so much better. Was that my magic again?

So cool.

My eyes snap open. Oh shit! That enormous monster. Malicious' house. Malicious!

His agonized voice comes from above me, his lips pressed to my hair. "I'm sorry. I'm sorry."

Wrapping my arms around him, I stroke his wings.

His chest shudders on a sob, and he hugs me tighter. "Summer, oh gods, Summer. I thought ..."

"Are you okay? Is it gone? What was that?"

Mal keeps me in his arms but leans back enough to look at my face. He stares at me, tears making his silver eyes shine even brighter. "That was an ancient. They usually keep to themselves, but I ..." I stroke his back as he swallows, dipping his head. "I messed up."

I press a kiss to his chest, and he sighs with a shiver. "Let me guess. The gem you mentioned before?"

I feel him nod. Looking around as much as I can, I take in the destruction. "Oh, your poor house." He waves me off, and I press a finger under his chin, lifting his gaze to meet mine. "Are you sure you're okay? You shielded me, and—" As he lifts his hand to cup my face, I notice the blackened skin of his palm, and is that bone? I grab his hand, careful to avoid the burns. "Oh my god, Malicious!"

As I stare at his charred hand, the black edges flake and fall away, his skin knitting together until all the damage is healed. He rests his palm against my cheek, his thumb brushing back and forth as he says, "I'm fine, Summer. And I'm so very sorry. I promised you'd be safe, and mere hours later, you almost die. You would have if not for your magic. I am unworthy of you. I can't—"

I pull myself to him, pressing my lips to his. I kiss along his mouth, determined to break through the hard, tense press of his lips. I kiss his cheek, his jaw, this throat, and by the time I get back to his mouth, he groans, finally opening for me.

We devour each other, riding the adrenaline of surviving the ancient, of being alive and in each other's arms. Malicious stands, shifting me so I can wrap my legs around his waist. We pepper each other with kisses as he picks his way through the wreckage. He has to flap his wings to carry us over the worst of the rubble. With the roof gone, the stars wink overhead, and I repress a shudder of fear as I recall how the ancient's body had completely blocked out the sky.

Mal carries me into the room in the back of his ruined home. His bedroom. There's still a small portion of the ceiling intact, and amazingly, as if protected by fate, his bed stands unscathed.

The room rotates as I fall. We fall together. Soft velvet caresses my back as we land on his bed. Tucking his wings, Mal looms over me, his thighs shoving my legs wide. His cock is back at my entrance, and I arch into him. My lips fall open as he squeezes my throat, sliding his length into me so slowly, I feel every stretched inch. He whispers, "You are my light, my joy. You are a breeze on a hot day. You are the sun breaking through the clouds after days of rain."

He bottoms out. Pleasure explodes like a sparkler, sizzling tingles erupting across my body. My orgasm flashes so suddenly and violently, I don't have time to scream. My back spasms from the deep arch of my body as I ride the bliss.

My vision comes back into focus as the shockwaves begin to ebb, but then Mal moves. Slow, rolling thrusts drive my orgasm back to its peak. I'm on a cresting wave that feels like it will never reach the shore. Mal curls around me, his hips driving his cock inside me in a delicious rhythm as he says, "You are so beautiful coming on my cock, mate. My mate." He presses his chest to mine, and we both groan as the vibrations of his growl shiver throughout my entire body. "I love you."

His wings flare out, curving around us, the feathers of one cupping the top of my head, the other draping over the side of the bed. I'm surrounded by him. It's a beautiful moment. It's overwhelming. But it's more than his physical body. Everything that is Malicious, consumes me.

I moan, "Malicious. My mate."

His pace picks up, and I cry out, another orgasm spiraling through me. He keeps me flying by grinding his pelvis against my clit with rolling thrusts. I'm sweaty and soaked from my arousal. I'm blissed out, and my muscles are beginning to shake, but I want to watch Malicious as he falls apart.

Wrapping my arms around him, I shudder as his feathers gently scrape against my skin. Lifting my head, I press my lips to his ear. "Malicious, I want to see what my mate looks like when he comes inside me."

He releases my neck, threading his arms under me. He hugs me so tightly, it's almost hard to breathe as he pumps into me, the wet sounds of our bodies slapping together accompanied by our gasps and moans and his growls. Malicious buries his face in my neck, chanting I think more to himself than to me. "Thank you. Thank you. Fates, thank you. T-thank ... you."

Tears roll down my cheeks as I'm overwhelmed by his words. I hug him as tightly as I can as everything crashes over me ... realizing how close we came to death. My fingers dig into the muscles of his back as I whisper, "I'm here. I've got you. Yes, Malicious, yes. You feel so good. Just like that. Please." My body coils again, and I clench around him as yet another climax approaches. "Malicious, I'm so close. Please. Please ..."

Pressing his forearms into the mattress on either side of my face, he lifts just enough to look into my eyes. They glow like silver moonlight on a calm lake. He thrusts into me once, twice, then holds himself deep, grinding and rolling his hips against me as he comes.

He's more glorious than I could have imagined. He

keeps his intense, bliss-filled gaze on me as he grits his teeth. His growl intensifies, vibrating the entire bed. The heat of his release fills me, and an obscene moan floats from my lips as my orgasm unfolds slowly but with so much intensity, my toes cramp as they curl with pleasure. I've never actually felt a man spend inside me before, but I do now as Mal's pulsing release hits my inner walls, driving my climax even higher.

His thrusts slow, and some of his seed leaks out, dripping down my already slick thighs. I'm sure we've ruined his velvet bedding.

Oh well, it goes with the rest of his destroyed house.

CHAPTER 16

MALICIOUS

In all my years of existence, I never dreamed being with my mate would feel so ... perfect. My thumbs trace along her cheekbones as she stares up at me. Her short hair is wild and damp with her sweat. Our bodies are still pressed together, my cock slowly softening inside her. I could stay like this for hours. I'd spend every drop of my magic to keep from having to leave her side.

Wiggling slightly under me, Summer's lips lift, and I feel the warmth of her smile all the way to my soul. Her voice is a little scratchy. "I'm sticky."

I chuckle, unable to recall the last time I was this happy. Shifting my hips, I reluctantly slide out of her, momentarily mesmerized as my cum seeps from her. I sit back on my heels as she lifts to brace herself on her elbows. Cocking her head to the side, she looks at the painting on the wall still somehow hanging over my headboard.

"Is that a Raphael?"

A pleased hum slides from my lips. "You know your art."

"Only the famous ones." She shifts again, and I move out of her way as she sits up and tucks one knee up to her chest. "Which one is that?"

"*St. Michael Vanquishing Satan.*"

She studies the painting. "It's dark, but ..."

"But?"

Peeking back at me, she smirks. "Is that supposed to be you?"

I shrug, matching her smirk.

She scoots to face me, and I love that she's unconcerned by her nudity because I love the view. Her fingers pinch the bedding as she says, "You've been around for so long. You've seen and experienced so much. I feel ..."

When she remains silent for a few long heartbeats, I take her hand, rubbing my thumb over her knuckles. "What is it, sunshine?"

She sighs. "I just feel stupidly young and naive. I feel inadequate."

Summer is so small, it's easy to scoop her into my lap. I wrap one hand around the back of her neck, and the other feathers along her side. Goosebumps prickle along her flesh as her eyes shutter at my touch. So perfect.

Pressing a quick kiss to her lips, I meet and hold her gaze. "Yes, I have been around for a long, long time. And in all that time, I have yearned, waited, raged, despaired, and sometimes even forsaken the idea of finally finding my mate." Summer bites her bottom lip, her eyes shimmering with tears ... for me? I push on, needing her to understand. "And now that I've found you, my Summer, my sunshine, my life, my mate, I realize all my imaginings, all my hopes, all my desires fell short. I've barely scratched the surface of knowing you, but I'm absolutely certain there has never been, nor will there ever be anyone more perfect for me than you."

A single tear escapes the corner of one of her eyes and trails down her cheek to drip into her lap. She wipes at her face before more tears can fall. A soft, emotional chuckle bursts from her mouth. "Well, what am I supposed to say to that?"

My wings curl around her, cocooning us. My lips press to hers, and she sighs into me. We continue to kiss, light, and soft, and gentle. We take comfort from each other. When I pull back slightly, I press my wings to her back, loving the way her bare skin feels against my feathers.

An idea pops in my head. "What would be your top destination of somewhere you've always wanted to go?"

She blinks up at me, her eyes skipping between mine. "That's a hard one."

I grin, pressing her to my hardening cock. She giggles, tapping one of her nails to my chest. "It seems angels don't need much recovery time."

Grinding her a little harder against me. "*I* don't need recovery time, not with my mate in my lap." She opens her mouth, but before she can respond, I say, "My question, Summer."

"Right. Yes. Okay. Let me think." She's only silent for a moment before she says, "Amami Oshima."

"The Japanese island?"

She nods and I smile, delighted I'm able to give my mate something she's always wanted. "Done."

Her eyes go wide. "What?"

Wrapping us in my magic, I pull us into the ether, slipping through space. If humans knew how to manipu-

149

late magical power to do this, they would call it a worm-hole, similar to their Einstein-Rosen bridge theory. A few lazy flaps of my wings carry us to our destination.

My toes sink into pristine sand as I let Summer slide down the front of my body. I keep her in the circle of my wings as she turns. She gasps as she looks out over the turquoise sparkling water. The Divide is still down, and it's morning on this side of the world. Soft, golden rays of sunshine gild the waves.

One of Summer's small hands grips the edge of my wing, and I can't help but press my body against hers, pleased as she leans into me. There's wonder in her voice, and my chest expands with pride as she says, "How did we ... Are we really ... This is ..."

I chuckle, wrapping my arms around her naked body. "Try to finish one of those questions."

She laughs. "Okay. Did you really just casually bend space and time to bring me to Japan?"

I rest my chin on her head. "Space, not time."

She shakes with her laugher. "This is amazing, Malicious. Thank you."

My lips press to her hair as I inhale our combined scents on her skin. "Well, you *are* on vacation."

She sighs again. Having my content mate in my arms might be the best feeling in the world.

Suddenly, she tenses, and I snap my magic around us, searching for any sign of a threat. Her grip on my wing tightens. "The Divide. I shouldn't be—"

My chuckle cuts her off. "Oh, sweet sunshine. There's no need to worry. Your mate is more than capable of keeping you safe." *Unless the ancient comes back. But I don't think we need to worry about him now that he has what he wants. I hope.*

She melts, resting her head against my chest. "I can't

believe we're on Amami Oshima right now." The volcanic mountains surround us, the water sparkles, and Summer wiggles her toes in the white sand. "This is unbelievable."

Releasing my mate, I spread my wings, lifting a few feet off the ground. Summer looks up at me with a question in her eyes, and I grin at her. "There's a cave at the far end of this beach." She looks over her shoulder then back at me. My skin starts to glow, and my cock stands erect against my stomach in anticipation. Will my little sunshine play with me? I growl for her. "Run."

She grins, only hesitating a second as her pupils dilate. Sand kicks up behind her as her toned legs flex with each sprint. She's small, but fast. I'm distracted by the way her ass bounces and the sexy ripple of her back muscles as she pumps her arms.

Fuck, she's glorious.

I hover, entranced as the morning sun kisses my mate's bare skin with golden light. Not even a nepha can compare to the beauty of my mate.

I realize she's already more than halfway down the beach. My cock weeps pre-cum, my core aching and throbbing with the need to be inside her, to claim her. I flap my wings twice, then spread them wide, catching a current. Swooping after her, the angle of the sun keeps my approaching shadow from crossing her vision, so she has no warning as I silently dive.

Her breath whooshes from her as I wrap my arms around her, taking her to the sand. She bucks in my hold, grunting, "No!"

I freeze. Has she misread the intention of my game?

Summer digs her feet into the sand, lurching out from under me. She takes off again, whooping with a happy war cry. "Ha! I won't lose! You'll never catch me!"

Ah. My grin nearly splits my face. Seems my mate has

a competitive streak. Her laughter dances on the ocean breeze as she sprints away from me. The chase is back on. Folding my wings, I relish the gritty feel of the sand sliding against the bottoms of my feet as I run after her. The occasional spray of salt water flecks against my skin, and as the sun continues to rise, heat warms the air.

I've never felt more alive.

She's within my grasp, and I reach for her with my hands and my magic. As soon as my power touches her, it ... dissipates. I'm so shocked, I stumble, losing precious space between us as Summer keeps running. Did she just repel my magic?

Wicked witch.

I'm on her in seconds. I've hit her hard, but even with my weight on her, she struggles, still trying to win. I'm so hard, it's painful. This is amazing. She is amazing.

Clawing at the sand, she throws an elbow, and I barely duck out of the way in time to avoid a bruised nose. I grab her shoulder, flipping her and pinning her with a palm to her chest. Still, she struggles. She's covered in sand, her legs kicking, but there's a ghost of a smile on her lips.

Wrapping her in my arms, I toss her over my shoulder and walk towards the water. She pinches my side, and I smack her with my wing, earning a burst of laughter from her. Once I'm waist deep, I dump Summer into the ocean. Her arms and legs wave, splashing frantically as her head breaks the surface. Water sputters from her lips as she coughs. When she gets her feet under her, the water laps at the underside of her breasts.

That's *my* job.

Crouching, I lift Summer back into my arms, and her legs wrap around my waist. I nuzzle into her neck. "I win."

She giggles, rubbing the front of her body against mine. Flaring my wings, I lift us out of the water and fly backwards towards the shore. My toes hit the sand, and I kneel. With my wings spread wide to avoid crushing them, I lay back. Summer straddles me, the wind ruffling her short hair, the sun highlighting her green eyes. Her skin glistens with water.

I sigh, tracing my hand down the front of her body. "Beautiful."

She shivers, gripping my length. "I vaguely recall you saying something about your cock doing ... things?"

I smirk, gripping her hips. "Indeed. Let me show you what your mate can do for you."

She rises, lining herself up, then torturously slowly lowers herself on my cock until I've filled her completely. We both groan as she grinds her hips, rubbing her clit on my pelvis. I cup her breasts, running my thumbs over her tight nipples before pinching them. Her head falls back, and her pussy clenches me as she moans, "Yes, Malicious."

She bounces and grinds on top of me, chasing her climax. My own pleasure curls tighter, and I'm already close. Sheer force of will keeps my orgasm at bay as I wrap my hands around her waist, controlling her pace, thrusting into her from the bottom.

"Are you ready for more?"

She nods, then gasps with a flush as she looks to where we're joined. A bronze light glows from my cock, already glistening with her arousal. The light is visible through her stomach, and little beams leak from her pussy.

She rides me harder, arousal pouring from her as she pants, "Mal, what ...?"

I thrust, then retreat, pulling out as I send my magic

to my cock. She gasps again as my length begins to pulse with expanding rings that roll up and down my cock. I smile as she wraps her fingers around me. I nearly come in her hand as she strokes me.

With a flex of her thighs, I'm back inside her. Her head falls back as I thrust into her, the vibrating rings of my cock stroking her inner walls. My magic heats my skin, the light growing brighter, seeping out of the space where we're joined.

Her voice stutters as I lick her neck. "Oh, Malicious. This is ... you are ... Oh my ... fuuuuuck."

Crushing her against me, I control myself long enough to press an open-mouthed kiss to the tempting skin where her shoulder and neck meet. She moans, tilting her head farther to the side, giving more access. My teeth close, biting softly, and when her pussy clenches and flutters around me, I deepen my growl and intensify the pulsing waves pushing the rings up and down my cock.

"Come for me, mate."

Her scream breaks on a cry of pure bliss. As she falls apart, I bite, hard. Summer rides me harder, spurred on by the pleasure/pain of my claiming. My jaw flexes until I break skin. Her blood barely touches my tongue, and I explode. The force of my climax is so powerful, I black out. All I feel is Summer, her taste, her power, her arousal, her voice screaming with pleasure ...

Magic fills me to bursting, and it's my own light shimmering from my skin that brings me back. My bronze light surrounds us as our eyes meet. Her pussy continues to squeeze me, and my orgasm lingers with shuttering tingles. Summer rises and falls on my cock slowly, her whispered words brushing against my mouth. "How do I ...?"

I kiss her, licking her lips before asking, "What? What do you need, mate?"

Her pussy grips me tighter as I call her mate, and renewed arousal fills me. She manages to say between gasps, "How do I claim you?"

Oh, fuck me. This woman is perfection.

I don't know if humans can claim monsters, but I want her to try. "Do what feels right."

Without hesitation, her palm lands on my chest. I feel it. I feel her. Her magic surges, curling through me, dancing with mine, intertwining until our powers are woven together like a tapestry. When I look at the place where her hand touches my chest, I marvel at the scrolling design that spreads up to my shoulder. It's beautiful, dark bronze curling lines with leaves and sunbursts.

I press my palm against the back of her hand. "Yes, Summer. Claim me. Mark me so all will see that I am yours."

With a cute little growl, she picks up her grinding pace, squeezing and sucking me with every roll of her body. Her head falls back, and with a feral grunt, I slam deep inside her, closing my mouth over my bite mark on her neck, sucking and licking.

We come together, our bodies trembling, our dual shouts pulled away by the breeze. Absolute bliss touches every inch of my body, inside and out. My wings have never taken me so high.

As the world comes back into focus, Summer rests her head on my chest, her fingers tracing little circles around her mark now tattooed on my skin. My own mark sits red and bruised on her. It's beautiful.

I stand, sliding out of her to cradle her sweet body in my arms. Nuzzling into her hair, crusty with sand and salt, I ask, "Is my mate happy?"

With a contented sigh, she presses a kiss to my chest. "Very." She chuckles. "Best summer vacation ever."

THE END

Catch the final novella in this series with the feared and mysterious
ancient and his mate.

Hunted on Halloween
Coming Fall 2024

ALSO BY T. B. WIESE

I genuinely hope you enjoyed this series. If you're interested, here are my other books - all adult fantasy with varying levels of spice.

Scan the code below for links to my Amazon author page where you'll find all my other books.

You'll also find a link to my website for signed paperbacks & hardcovers as well as swag.

ACKNOWLEDGMENTS

A huge thank you to my readers. Without you, this crazy dream of being an author would not be possible.

To all my beta & ARC readers, thank you! You had a big hand in making this series what it is today. Thank you so very much for taking the time to help me polish this story.

And lastly, I want to thank all my friends and family for cheering me on and being as excited about my characters as I am—I love my tribe.

ABOUT THE AUTHOR

T. B. Wiese is a military spouse, dog mom, photographer, Disney nerd, and lover of spicy fantasy. She loves animals (She grew up with dogs and working with horses, including working at the Tri-Circle D Ranch at Disney World), so don't be surprised when you find yourself reading lovable animal characters in her novels.

If you'd like to keep up to date with future releases as well as new swag and sales, sign up for her newsletter via link in code below.

SCAN THE CODE WITH YOUR CAMERA APP FOR HER SOCIAL LINKS

Printed in Great Britain
by Amazon

45279293R00099